God, Grace, Dumb Luck

PHLOYD KNUCKLEZ

ISBN: 0692780998
ISBN-13: 978-0692780992

DEDICATION

To Sol from Jersey. You don't know who the hell he is but if you had
written a book you would have dedicated to him, too.

ACKNOWLEDGMENTS

Forget exactly what ya'll did, but I'm pretty sure you did something. At least I hope you did. So, anyway, I'm acknowledging you. Just noticed you're all females. Hmm. Interesting.

Abby Hebert
Arlene Burt
Autumn Marilyn Foster
Bianca Mcclain
Carly Elvia Travis
Claire Bridget Macdonald
Darlene Everett
Diann Juliette Gamble
Edith Matthews
Felecia Reilly
Ginger Jenna Hunter
Gloria Lillian Adkins
Gloria Walton
Helena Grant
Janet Earlene Santos
Jeannette Lynda Wagner
Jennie Hutchinson
Jodi Williams
Jodie Ruth Blackwell
Joni Copeland
Karina Marina Ferguson
Keri Angelica Jennings
Kristen Dickson
Lakeisha Cameron
Leann Dorsey
Leanna Casandra Kim
Leona Ortiz
Lorraine Jennifer Alvarez
Maggie Tanya Wall
Marcella Conley
Margarita Randi Mcleod
Melisa Roth

Melissa Stevens
Nanette Millie Robles
Nola Adriana Pickett
Pam Morgan
Rosemarie June Briggs
Rosetta Esperanza Stevens
Ruth Padilla
Sarah Harrison
Sheila Howell
Shelia Drake
Sheri Neva Blackburn
Susanne Mitzi Lindsay
Sybil House
Tabitha Elliott
Tanisha Celina Whitley
Tracie Celia Deleon
Trina Marquez
Yolanda Jennifer Cash

Part Of The Unraveling Process

It seems these days people are more interested
in talking about themselves
than in listening to anything I have to say.

Now maybe that's because what I have to say isn't
all that interesting or isn't relevant to their lives or maybe
I've just been talking to the wrong people.

I realize I'm not the most charismatic guy in the world;
if you looked at me at all, it would probably be because
you were about to bump into me
and if you did happen to bump into me
and you were in a particularly charitable frame of mind
you might apologize or excuse yourself.

On the other hand, if you were in a hurry
and on your way to meet a much more substantial person,
you might mutter something angrily under your breath
and question my navigational skills or think I was
just another clumsy daydreamer or drunken vagrant.

Not that being so forgettable is not without its advantages.

For instance, nobody will ever look at me and call me a leader.
Or yearn for any of my belongings.
Or fantasize about what kind of lover I'd be.
Or wonder if I'd make a good husband and father.
Or want to pick a fight with me.
Or pray for my salvation.
Or bargain for my soul.
Or lay their head on my shoulder.
Or recruit me to join an adult softball league.
Or ask me for money.
Or solicit an opinion from me.
Or seek my advice.
Or need me to do anything at all, really,

except maybe get the hell out of their way
so we can both go our separate ways.

The Subtleties Have Yet To Flesh Themselves Out

Jhonny came marching home from Iraq, armed with a bottle of Chivas Regal and a gun, the same day Sally was released from rehab.

And when Jhonny arrived on Sally's doorstep with a bouquet of flowers that badly needed watering, Sally kissed him on the cheek, anyway, without making him feel like a shrinking violet.

And when they were sitting on the couch later that night sipping scotch and parsing the importance of good personal hygiene, Sally looked into Jhonny's ears and said, "Do you ever clean them?"

And Jhonny, always sheepish about such things, admitted, "I don't. I just hope the water from the shower cleans them out."

And Sally laughed so hard she felt like she had a lack of oxygen and the fatigue she'd been experiencing for several months began to affect her again in a way she couldn't quite explain. "It's somewhere between heavy resignation and heavy lifting," said Sally.

And Jhonny, who'd been suffering from the difference between having fun and having none, just smiled as he wrote out a check to Sally, instructing her not to cash it until his boat came in. [His boat was currently bobbing somewhere out there on one of the better-known oceans, "like a burnt cork," he liked to say, but it was on its way into shore, he was sure of that; he knew the captain personally and he was "a good man," although he drank every other day, especially during high tide, but Jhonny insisted that Jesus was on his side, because "Jesus is like that sometimes."]

And Sally, who was "so tired of taming her tongue," could only stare into her tumbler of scotch and wonder how much longer she would have to wait before the alcohol made her feel like she could "feel her flesh again."

And as Jhonny struggled to read some of the vocabulary in Sally's body language, which was usually on about an eleventh grade reading level, he asked Sally if she would provide him with some CliffsNotes before continuing their discussion; however, Sally politely explained to him that she had already dumbed-down her curriculum enough for Jhonny and if he "wasn't willing to put in the time to study more," she would simply have to flunk him for the semester, which caused a sick feeling in Jhonny's throat, followed by the thought that his life had turned into a depraved nightmare of paranoia, excess drinking, disillusionment, and a rage that might one day land him jail for life.

And as Jhonny recalled the tall tales of his childhood, his early years in an orphanage, adoption and a stint in military school, where he was expelled for writing a short play titled "What's Yours is Mine," a satire about Jesus' life as a carpenter, in which he portrayed Jesus and St. Joseph, the patron saint of carpenters, as con artists running a "home repair" scam on seniors, he drifted off to sleep.

And Sally opened her journal and wrote the following entry: "I escaped the ghetto of my environment but I didn't escape the ghetto of my soul."

And she walked out on Johnny forever, virtually untouched.

Sunstruck

I was fifteen and we had these neighbors. The Hanson's. Mrs. Hanson sunbathed in the backyard in a bikini rubbing baby oil all over her every fifteen minutes.

My bedroom window was situated in such a way that, with the aid of binoculars, I could see everything. I'd be up there watching her and every time, and every time, without fail, she'd drop her top, so her tits could tan.

I'm this fifteen-year-old punk with raging hormones.

One day my mother walks in on me.

"WHAT ARE YOU LOOKING AT? WHY DO YOU HAVE THOSE BINOCULARS? WHO'S OUT THERE?"

And I'm bullshittin' her, right, I'm like, "I'm bird-watchin', Ma, I'm lookin' for cracks in the roof, lookin' for signs of termites," anything I can think of.

She looks out the window, sees Mrs. Hanson, goes ballistic. "HOW COULD YOU…WHY DID YOU… HORRIBLE, SHAMEFUL, SINFUL, IMMORAL…VIOLATING MRS. HANSON'S PRIVACY…YOU COULD GO TO JAIL FOR THIS…MY SON THE PERVERT," on and on.

Naturally, she calls Mrs. Hanson. Says she has some very disturbing news regarding me, could the three of us meet to discuss the problem, blah blah blah.

So she drags me over to the Hanson's. I'm thinking, "God, please don't let Mr. Hanson be there, please, if you have any mercy at all…"

Mrs. Hanson's got this look on her face like "What the fuck's going on?"

And my mother, very dramatically, like right out of Colombo or some shit, produces the binoculars, like she had just found the murder weapon, right, and says to Mrs. Hanson, I'll never forget it, it still reverberates in my mind to this day. "My son was spying on you through these while you were sunbathing and became aroused." Became aroused! And then goes into a twenty minute diatribe on the declining morals and values and scruples of the youth of America.

I'm standing there like a schmuck, completely humiliated, stripped of all pride and dignity, while Mrs. Hanson's got this frozen look of shock and embarrassment on her face.

Suddenly a car drives up. And who decides to come home from lunch that day? Mr. Hanson. Yeah, and he's a little edgy that day, a little cranky. The veins in his neck are throbbing and he's lookin' like he's about to suffer an aneurism and my mom's about to tell him I got hot for his wife.

Fortunately, Mrs. Hanson, sensing eminent doom, improvises brilliantly by telling my mother she was sure it was just an innocent mistake and that we should just forget the whole thing.

Okay, great.

Now lemme tell you a little something about my mother. My mother likes a good payoff. She doesn't like things swept under the carpet. She thrives on confrontations and their consequences.

So Mr. Hanson approaches us, sweating, grumbling, bitching, acknowledging my mother and I with a grunt. He looks at his wife, at my mother, at me, his wife again.

"What's goin' on?" he says.

"Oh, nothing," Mrs. Hanson says with a forced smile.

Long, awkward, dramatic pause. And it's moments like that when my mother really shines. Only this time she didn't go in for the kill. Instead. And this really blew my mind because my mother actually lied for me, which was unheard of. She thanks Mrs. Hanson for finding my binoculars, since I had recently developed such an appreciation for bird watching and we say our goodbyes, go back home.

Fast forward a few years.

I'm out of school for the summer; mowing the lawn. My shirt's off, getting a little tan, feeling good. I look out of the corner of my eye. Mrs. Hanson is sunbathing in her backyard, watching me through a pair of binoculars and giving me the thumbs up! I'm, like, holy Jesus, talk about full circle!

Then Mr. Hanson comes out of the house, walks toward me, hands me a beer, says, "I owe you a debt of gratitude, my friend…"

I'm like, "What for?"

He says, "It took a fifteen year old kid to make me see just how attractive my wife really is. Our sex life has never been better. Thanks, pal…"

He shakes my hand, gives me a little wink, and walks away.

The Deepest Need

Elijah Fitzgerald was last seen conversing with Myrtle Rucker at that party in Chelsea.

"I went through est in 1973," said Elijah. "Do you know what est is?"

"Uhmm…"

"Surely you've heard of est. Erhard Something Training… yeah…and what I learned from that experience is that Life Only Consists Of This Moment… not the past, not the future, not yesterday, not tomorrow… and the other thing I learned was I can create for good or ill… do you know what I mean?"

"Oh, yes," Myrtle said.

"I have the option of doing good things or doing bad things…" Elijah shrugged, took a sip of his Manhattan, and tamped a Chesterfield out of the pack.

"Interesting," said Myrtle, trying to guess his fatal flaw. "You're married? I don't mean to pry…"

"No," Elijah said. "But there's actually an interesting story behind that… I errr… was supposed to be married…I was engaged to be married… but the girl, the woman, I should say, whom I was engaged to was schizophrenic…Long story short, she killed herself… "

"Oh, no," Myrtle said.

"It was unfortunate… I-I-I- basically blame myself…She went into the garage, got into the car…Obviously, carbon monoxide poisoning…she was very special to me… she was about the only woman I was ever friendly with, in addition to being her…" He cleared his throat nervously. "…lover, of course, errr." He suppressed a few tears and choked a bit. "I say I blame myself," he continued… "I'm not supposed to blame myself. My doctor says I'm not supposed to do that; she says it was her own doing and I'm not responsible for her actions and this and that and… Conceptually, she may be right…Emotionally, you know, that's a whole other story… Anyway, uhmm… I am single, however, I…" He couldn't find the thread of the thing he was trying to say. "I was gonna say something…" He shook his head and shrugged. "I've completely forgotten…"

"Uh-huh," Myrtle said, feigning interest.

"So," Elijah said. "Are you single?"

"Mm hmm."

Elijah slapped himself. "Listen; don't pay any attention to me…I'm…very nervous… I'm sweating… Basically, I'm a basket case, in case you haven't noticed…" He pulled at his shirt sleeve near his shoulder.

"I think you're an interesting person," Myrtle said, watching Elijah's little nervous tick.

"In what way?" Elijah said.

"You seem very bright."

"Really? I try to be…"

That's when Myrtle was approached by a tall, good-looking man with a submissive grin.

"Would you excuse me?" Myrtle said to Elijah.

"Uhm, maybe I could call you sometime," Elijah said. "We could have a…"

"Have you eaten yet?" the good-looking man said to Myrtle.

"No, I was waiting for you," Myrtle said.

"Oh, aren't you wonderful," the man said.

Then Myrtle turned to Elijah. "It was nice meeting you…good luck."

"Thank you," Elijah said. "I actually could probably use some…"

Myrtle and her companion headed for the buffet as Elijah stood by himself, waiting for some other kind of refuge.

An Intimate Relationship Which Should Never Be Broken

My poem is about you.

It's a fiction that unfolds marvelously.

Simple and unaffected.

Ancient and powerful.

Not nihilistic.

Or dismal.

Or apocalyptic.

Sexy.

Enlightened.

Essentially honest in your actions,
predominantly defiant
in the present tense,
you juggle manmade and science,
language and character,
stories and sensations.

There's something chemical about that.

To Plunder And Misrepresent

I hadn't worked in, like, a year. I was living on unemployment. I'd get calls from friends and family members.

"Found a job yet?"

"Not yet."

"What's going on?"

I always resented that question. I didn't think it was appropriate under the circumstances. I'd play it off. "It's hard out there," I'd tell them. "Economy's in rough shape."

"Well, hell, there's always McDonald's."

Right…

Fortunately, I knew how to hustle. Every now and then I'd run into lonely spinsters who would offer to cook for me. We'd have insane conversations. They'd tell me all about their cats, their birds, their overdue library fines. I'd just nod and smile, and excuse myself after tea.

"You could stay here," they'd say. "I've got a spare bedroom."

I'd thank them, tell them I've made other arrangements.

"Other arrangements?" they'd say.

"Yes, ma'am," and leave it at that.

When times got tough, I'd call up old girlfriends, and sleep on their couches. They'd play the games they played as kids and I'd watch them from a safe distance. Some would light incense, others would do yoga, but they'd all end up telling me why they broke up with me.

"You're strangely distant and emotionally unavailable."

"You're a drifter, a loner, lazy, self-absorbed and unambitious."

"You're afraid of responsibility and pressure."

Then I'd go home, enroll in some correspondence course in locksmithing or gunsmithing or small business management, earn a certificate, and trot it around to potential employers.

They'd look at me, smirk really, try to make me feel inadequate.

"I've dealt with my share of tragedy and heartbreak," I'd tell them.

They'd shake their heads, light a cigarette, take personal phone calls.

"No, I don't like that color for the upstairs bedroom, goddammit, now, how many times do I have to tell you, fuchsia is not appropriate!"

They'd hang up, wouldn't apologize, would just go on with the interview.

"Sooo… what is your greatest strength?"

I'd yawn and twitch a little.

"My greatest strength is I punch every button people got."

They'd go, "Uh heh, mm hmm, interesting," take another personal call.

"The curtains don't match the carpet! They must match the carpet, for chrissakes! Feng shui, feng shui!"

They'd slam the phone down. "God, people are so stupid " they'd say.

I'd usually agree with them, and ask about the salary requirements of the job.

"Son, I'll keep your resume on file."

"Okay."

Then I'd leave, say to myself, "what the fuck," and go to my bank and take another cash advance on my credit card and catch a movie or go to IHOP.

Pawning Her Dignity

She lived in an attic apartment above a drycleaner in the red light district of a city whose inhabitants walked around muttering to themselves and pulling punches whenever they weren't busy getting tired of waiting around for absolutely nothing.

One day, while feeling somewhat virtuous after dropping a quarter into a blind man's cup on the anniversary of St. Peter's imprisonment and deliverance, she suddenly recalled a proverb she'd learned in catechism years ago:

"If you see a blind man, kick him. Why should you be kinder than God?"

She remembered the sister explained it something like this: "In other words, if somebody suffers, God must have had a good reason for making them suffer."

"But what kind of God would do a thing like that?" she asked the sister.

The sister gave her a stern look. "Child, you are in no position to question God's will. You can go to hell for asking questions like that. You must learn how to be so comforted. Are you comforted by Jesus? Do you go to church and say I'm not very bright, but I do believe that you are the son of God. I do believe You died for me, Lord.' Do you do that?"

"Whoops," she said. "You got me there, sister," and the following week, she became a Buddhist.

A World Of Paperboys

The paperboy,
who's late as usual,
scans the headlines.

Even though his route
size has grown,
not everybody subscribes.

By the time he finishes
delivering the papers,
the corrections outnumber the

facts and the facts
yellow with time,
but the paperboy remains a boy.

A Real Natural Passionate Act

I went away somewhere
in my head and just stayed there
until you came along and said,

"You must be turning over some
well intriguing and provocative
problem in there…what are you grappling with?"

I was still.

You said, "If there was something you
wanted to say, what would it be?"

I took a sip of my Riesling and said,
"That sense of being out there all alone
is a lifetime bond."

You said, "Dreams die hard."

I said, "I'm still in flux…still in flex."

You said, "You can't walk away from defeat.
Just like a cowboy can't run away from a gunfight."

Every atom in my body was just buzzing.

You said, "Everybody has a journey in life. Everybody
has a journey every day."

As I worked myself into you,
your split ends were
wrapped around my tongue.

It felt like
the ocean was bowing to us and
the waves were obeying my cock.

You motioned toward my neck with your
teeth and your breath reddened the skin
on my face,

but there was no sound between your thighs,
other than condensed air, and the crackling
fire inside this arsonist's heart.

As Vague As He Is Flawed

Failed poet said,

"I stopped taking my meds because I didn't like the way they made me feel. I walked around like a zombie, totally numb. What's the point? I'd rather be able to feel something, even if it's anger and despair and irritation and sadness. I'm a poet, I need to be able to experience the entire range of my emotions, that's like taking away an artist's paint and asking him to dip his brush into a pail of dishwater. How do you paint a sunset using dishwater? How do you write a poem if you can't feel anything? I slipped right into that role, too, so easily. The socially-awkward, misunderstood, self-conscious drunken loner. And it fit so snugly against my skin. That's the way they all were, I told myself, so I was like that. You can convince yourself of almost anything if you're willing to sacrifice certain aspects of yourself. It was a trap, I realize that now. But when you're twenty, twenty-one, what do you know about traps? Twenty-odd years later, the chickens have come home to roost."

Encouraging Soul said,

"What matters is, did you do your best? Do these poems embody your integrity and represent who you really are?"

Failed Poet said,

"To me they're just a lot of chatter that has nothing to do with reality."

Encouraging Soul said,

"I carry around this quote I read recently. About people who realize, rather bitterly, that they can't change the world and that righteousness and idealism have their limits. 'By the end of his life, a new man emerges: a man no longer interested in changing the universe but devoted to enriching his corner of the world'. It's helped me, anyway. I struggle every day of my life with anger and ask god to work it out for me. I used to tell people, 'I'm just keepin' it real. If you don't like it, I got no time for you, so bump you'. I wasn't angry at them. I was angry at myself. Mostly at the choices I'd made. For internalizing all those childhood labels and stereotypes. For being a people-pleaser. Being afraid to say no to family members. Submitting to men I had no business submitting to. Allowing them to make decisions for me, knowing full well they didn't have the intellectual capacity to make those decisions, but I didn't trust my own instincts, even though they were right. So I know all about chickens coming home to roost."

Failed Poet said,

"And a cliché becomes a cliché because more often than not they're true."

Encouraging Soul nodded as Failed Poet returned to the biggest myth in the history of myths.

The myth that if you get hurt, you crawl off the field.

If you can't crawl off the field, somebody will come get you.

No Help In Truth

My mom calls me.

"How are you?" she says.

"Fine," I say.

"Are you meeting anyone?"

"I meet people everywhere I go, Ma."

"What sort of people?"

"People."

"Whores and misfits?"

"Whores and misfits? Ma, what makes you think – how do you even know about whores and misfits?"

"Believe me, I know."

I sigh. "Dad there?"

"He's napping."

"Jesus, does he ever not nap?"

"Don't be fresh…Have you met any nice girls?"

"I meet a lot of nice girls."

"Who aren't whores?"

"I don't go out with whores."

"What about that Puerto Rican girl?"

"She was Dominican."

"Whatever…"

"She wasn't a whore."

"Are you still seeing her?"

"Noo…"

"Then she's a whore."

"Ma!"

"I know a whore when I see one."

"You never saw her."

"I didn't have to see her…I heard."

"What did you hear?"

"What I heard was sufficient."

"Ma…"

"What do you got against marriage?"

"Nothing."

"So why aren't you married?"

"I haven't found the right girl, yet…"

"Don't gimme that."

"Marriage is not for everyone."

"Spoken like a true misfit."

"I'm not a misfit!"

"What was the point of dropping out of school?"

"I wasn't learning anything."

"And what are you learning now?"

"I'm learning to stay away from home."

"Very funny."

"I'm not joking."

"You're a fresh boy."

"You want I should be stale?"

"You better tell better jokes than that in your act."

"Don't worry about my act."

"I blame your father."

"For what?"

"For being too soft.

"Ma…"

"He's always been soft."

"He's a man, he's got flaws, so what?"

"When are you coming home?"

"Never."

"Stop it."

"You think I'm joking?"

"I miss you."

"I miss you, too."

"When?"

"Always."

"Now that you should put in your act."

"One day, I swear to God, Ma, you're gonna be proud of me."

"I should live that long? Don't hold your breath."

"How come our conversations are so antagonistic?"

"Because you're fresh and you're unresolved."

I laugh. "Unresolved?…Jesus Christ, when your mother says you're unresolved…"

"Goodbye, sonny."

"Ma?"

"What?"

"Love you."

"What else is new?"

Teach Me Your Ways

I was alone,
unemployed,
living on assistance from the United Way,
riding mass transit to job fairs,
eating ramen noodle soup and Kraft mac and cheese.

It was a fruitless existence.

No phone.

Then no electricity.

It was the middle of February.

I kept warm by wearing a snowsuit and
bundling myself in three wool blankets.

The only light came from trick candles
in a menorah and a Bugs Bunny night light.

My mailbox was filled with
threatening letters from my landlord,
my credit card companies.

Then a visit
from the sheriff's department.

Eviction notice.

Blah blah blah,
blah blah blah.

Walked to the bus stop,
on my way to the soup kitchen to get a
baloney sandwich and their soup du jour.

Met a woman named Goldy

who smiled at me, for some reason, and
struck up a conversation.

"You okay?" she said.

"I've been better," I said.

"You look tired," she said.

"I was born tired…"

She laughed, said she liked my sense of humor.

Told her I didn't think I was being all that funny.

She laughed some more.

Said I kind of reminded her of Paul Simon.

Wanted to know if I was a musician.

"Used to be," I said. "Long time ago…"

"What did you play?"

"Drums…"

"Ohmigod," she said. "I love drummers! Ya'll have so much rhythm!"

"Sometimes," I said.

She laughed again.
I wondered why she kept laughing.

I wasn't cracking any jokes.

She asked me if I was hungry.

"I am," I said.

"Do you like gumbo?"

"I do."

"I'll make you some tonight."

"Okay."

She was the one who began it all.

My journey.

My education.

My salvation.

I told her I wasn't a praying man,
she didn't give a damn,
just wanted me to kiss her
all over her body, and
we enjoyed ourselves immensely.

When she put her hands down my pants,
I sighed, and she loved that because it
was a joyful sigh, a sigh that told her she
was satisfying me completely.

I couldn't wait to make love to her,
couldn't wait till her mouth tasted me.

I looked into her beautiful eyes and never
lied to her, always told her what she
knew about herself;
predicted I would leave her
one day, and watched her as she resigned
herself to that reality.

But she never wavered in her devotion to me.

She believed I would make her life just a little
bit better for at least a moment or two and
that was enough for her.

It was more than anyone else had offered her.

She was so fragile, but tougher than me.

She wouldn't back down when I argued
with her ethics and her morals.

I couldn't hide my
unobtrusive nature
with her.

She couldn't hide her passion for dirty talk
with me.

Keeping My Vigil

Let me get something settled cause you're gonna hear all kinds of stories about me.

Yes, I am a fallen man.

I was tempted by the serpent and I believed him when he said the fruit of the Tree of Knowledge of Good and Evil would make me wise.

So now I'm surviving – by the sweat of my brow – condemned to live an ordinary, human life.

Just like you.

Forever questioning my own personal commitment, my own personal faith, my own personal salvation while still hoping to alter my life for the better and discover the truth about who I am and why I'm on this earth.

Even as an invisible force keeps me from being free to live my life.

Inexhaustible Blues

I pack my bags, move to West Hollywood among a cluster of homosexuals who don't hit on me.

My landlady is Israeli. She automatically assumes I'm anti-Semitic. I can tell by her suspicious smile. She refuses to shake my hand when we meet. Her husband tells me she's a germaphobe.

There's a garage band in the duplex next to mine carelessly playing the Dead Kennedys. After every song, the lead singer screeches into the mike, "That was bloody fucken awful!"

My upstairs neighbor is 77, a former screenwriter and member of the Communist Party. Says they hauled him in front of the House Un-American Activities Committee. "When they asked me if I was a commie-pinko," he says. "I told 'em to kiss my Marxist tuches…did a year in the Federal Corrections Institute in Danbury, Connecticut…" He falls asleep with a half-lit cigarette dangling from his bottom lip, muttering, "in this life, kid, you gotta have a platform…Gotta have a platform…"

After tucking him into bed, I go back to my place to view my Tia Chi instructional video.

Around midnight, a fight breaks out in the courtyard between a cordial cokehead and a reformed Catholic.

The old commie upstairs is shouting at them: "Neo-realism is a decidedly left-wing thing to do!"

The next morning, I receive a call from my germ phobic Israeli landlady.

"What was all the ruckus about?" she says.

"It was about platforms, Mrs. Zur. In this life you gotta have a platform…"

Mrs. Zur sighs, says, "Oy gevalt…farshtunkener," and hangs up.

Something Distinct And Challenging, All On Its Own

So now they're all holding rallies, thinking they're going to be the ones to set this country on fire again. But who's kidding whom? What do they really want? What does anybody *really* want? Love? Sex? Respect? Money? Power? Egos stroked until their ids come all over their superegos? It's a simple question. Costs a hell of a lot more than $64,000 these days, but I think you'll find the answer is reasonably priced. In fact, it might even be on sale. For the right asking price. Just call up your friendly neighborhood lobbyist; they're the ones hanging out in the lobby of the Ritz Carlton reading the Financial Times and having green tea and pastries.

And then the scene suddenly dissolves. But where are the network cameras? Out of focus again. But if you squint real hard you can see where the unemployment lines meet the coke lines and then you can watch them go to the after party with the thugs who can't be identified in a lineup because they have diplomatic immunity.

Where is America? Where is Miss America? Being raped by Captain America, of course.

And once again our judicial system has turned a blind eye to Lady Justice, who's grown tired of being in the dark and has removed her blindfold and replaced it with shades of gray.

All those cancerous witches and warlocks pretending to race for the cure by filling out their pledge forms; but they don't want to cure this disease. They want the disease to spread.

They want to create a pandemic that is voter-resistant. What rhetoric! What spin! What a disenchanted forest we've wandered into again. Waiting for Supermen like Zuckerberg and Gates to be the saviors of our public schools because all those demagogic demigods on our school boards are more concerned with rewriting the history of the world by filling our children's textbooks with ideological battles between Darwin and Christ.

"And, by the way, where is Christ in all this?" says the Atheist to the

Evangelical.

"Living in you," says the Evangelical.

"No, He's not," says the Atheist. "He's with all those other ubermensches who always seem to be reaching toward thrilling ideas only to suddenly abandon them."

And 'round and 'round the burning bush they go and where they stop, nobody knows; not even the shadow government knows what evil lurks inside the hearts and minds of the men and women of the Mad Tea Party who insist on seizing upon our differences and apprehensions rather than trying to grasp the reasons why the merry-go-round has collapsed mid-season.

A Rare Tolerance To The Future

It was a choice between "Birth of the Cool" and "A Love Supreme."

Nobody could make a decision.

They were all too busy complaining about their parents.

Eddie said, "My dad says to me, my father worked harder than me and I worked harder than you."

That was pretty much the way the rest of the evening unfolded.

Not enough ownership.

Too much projecting.

A guy who needed a haircut and a good fuck said, "Me, I love ugly girls…Pretty women can do anything… but ugly women have to do everything…"

Somebody's cell phone rang. Twenty people reached for theirs.

"Is it yours? Whose is it? Is that you?"

By the time the owner of the ringing phone answered it, the caller had hung up.

A tiny shrill voice shouted, "HEY LET'S PLAY SCATEGORIES!"

But nobody said anything.

Then the tiny shrill voice, now no more than a whisper, mumbled, "or not…"

Eddie started in on his dad again. "My father says, your sister has perseverance, your brother has perseverance, you're the only one who doesn't have perseverance…"

Everything that night was right down the middle.

By the time I'd left, they were memorializing each other.

Entropy had once again brought a roomful of people to their knees.

Preferring Form To Truth

My x-girl, with her hair getting twenty hours
of unstoppable volume and her face getting
the deepest-feeling clean available, just got
her PhD from Berkeley last month and now
she's driving a cab.
Her pops had to file
bankruptcy as a result of sending the
apple-of-his-astigmatic-eye through eight years
of "I'm not really sure what I wanna do."

Her moms said, "Well, she obviously lives in a
post love-in, post be-in kind of world."

I hear she's been going to clubs and getting
trashed a lot lately.

"I'm a fatalist," she once told me. "Most Irish
Catholics are like this. You play the hand you're
given and you do the best you can. If you're always
worried about, what if this happens, what if that
happens, then you miss the joy of life."

That was the night I lost it and spilled Jack Daniels
all over her trendy V-neck blouse and set fire to it and
flung it out the window.

"What in fuck's name were you thinking," she kept
yelling over and over. Then she threw a frozen pork chop
at me and knocked out two of my teeth, took my last Michelob,
flipped me off, and flagged a cab.

I didn't call her for two weeks.

When I attempted to extend the olive branch, I approached
her front door with a dozen red roses and an apology.

She wouldn't answer the door, even though I knew she was there.

At least her Acura was there and her cockapoo was cowering in
her doghouse and I could hear her stereo blasting Alanis Morissette.

The Country We Inhabited

The day after I barely graduated from high school, my father took me fishing.

I didn't really like to fish, but I had nothing else to do, so I figured what the hell?

The problem was as soon as we cast our rods, he said, "So what are your plans?"

Which was a question I really wasn't interested in answering at that point in my life.

So I didn't; which really pissed him off.

"Well?" he said.

 "Gimme a break, Dad…"

 That was all he needed to hear.

 "Give you a break?"

"Yeah…"

"Mmh. That was the wrong thing to say to me… that was the wrong thing to say to me…"

And then he launched into one of the longest speeches I've ever heard him or any other parent give.

It must have gone on for at least a half an hour.

I was kind of glad I'd forgotten my watch because otherwise I would have kept checking it every two minutes, wondering how much longer he was going to keep lecturing me, and that would have really pissed him off.

So I just looked straight ahead and pretended to give a damn about fishing.

Somewhere around the three-quarter mark of his speech, right after he'd finished listing all the sacrifices he and my mother had made for me over the last God-knows-how-many years, I felt a little tug on my fishing line.

"I think I got something," I said, but my father didn't hear me.

He was rambling on and on about how important it is to set goals and make plans for the future because before I'd know it, I'd be forty and I'd probably be filled with all kinds of regrets and disappointments and by then it would be too late and…

Christ, I get so tired whenever somebody lectures me.

I literally get sleepy and want to take a nap.

I sometimes think when people are lecturing you, they're really lecturing themselves.

I can't prove that theory, because I'm not a psychologist, but it's just something I've always thought.

Anyway, I was trying to focus on reeling in whatever the hell I'd hooked, which didn't seem like anything special.

Whatever it was, it wasn't putting up much of a fight.

"You know, the reality is," my father continued. "you won't have any idea of anything I'm saying until you have kids of your own… and at the rate you're going, I don't even see that happening…not unless you stop cockin' around, which I don't see happening either. I could be wrong; I hope I am."

Yada yada yada…

Well, turns out I didn't hook a fish at all.

"Looks like a bustier," my father said, examining it.

"A what?" I said.

"It's a woman's…"

That's as far as his explanation went.

"It's like underwear?" I said.

"Something like that…"

I didn't push it.

He obviously didn't want to discuss it in detail.

Which was fine with me.

I think it would have been awkward as hell talking to my father about bustiers, anyway.

I don't even think I could talk to him about my underwear.

That's how screwed-up our relationship was back then.

Okay, well, "screwed-up" might be a little strong.

If I can think of a better way to describe the relationship between my father and me at that time, I'll let you know.
Until then, I'm not going spend much time on it.

I've got more important things to do.

Like trying to figure out how the hell I'm going to spend the next forty years of my life.

Days Of Yawn

My old man had dragged me to Yom Kippur services.

Which was cool because I got to take the day off from school.

"The self-appointed big-mouth of the synagogue," (that's what my old man called him) was this crazy old Russian dude named Reuben.

Reuben must have been about eighty at the time.

Little guy, about five-three, maybe a hundred and twenty pounds.

But he was a feisty bastard.

Well, Ruben was holding up the service because he was waiting for Irving Cohen to arrive; he didn't want to start the service without a Cohen being present.

Something about how a Cohen is supposed to recite one of the blessings over the Torah.

I don't know, I'm not a biblical scholar, so I don't know what the hell it was all about.

But, anyway, my old man was furious.

First of all because everyone in town knew Irving was a drunk.

And not only was he a drunk, he was an Atheist, too.

And everyone knew this.

Including Reuben.

But it didn't matter to Reuben whether Irving was a drunk or an Atheist.

He was "A Cohen," and that was all that mattered.

That's when my old man got a hold of Reuben.

And things got ugly.

"This is ridiculous, Reuben," my old man said. "Why the hell are we sitting around here waiting for a loser like Irving?"

"I want a Cohen… Irving is the only Cohen in town…And we have no Levis…"

"Irving could give less than a crap about being a Cohen. Or this synagogue! Or you or anyone else! And we don't need either a Cohen or a Levi to recite the blessings… any one of us can recite the damn things!"

"Relax, we'll wait… if he doesn't come in a reasonable amount of time…"

"A reasonable amount of time? Services were supposed to start at nine o'clock. It's now nine-forty-five!"

"Patience, please…"

"Patience, my ass!"

"Please, no cursing…"

"This isn't about him being a 'Cohen' at all and you know it… This is about his goddamn money… You've always been impressed by money… and the rest of us just aren't good enough for you to get up there and recite the blessings… that's what it's about!"
"It's about tradition…"

"Oh bullshit! It is not! Reuben, you are such a hypocrite!"

That's when my old man grabbed me by the arm and we rushed out of the synagogue, forgetting to take our yarmulkes off.

Boy, he was pissed.

The whole way home, he just stewed.

After that, I knew we wouldn't be going to any more services.

And we didn't.

We observed the Jewish holidays, alright.

We just didn't observe them in a synagogue.

That's when my old man introduced me to horse racing.

And I've been a convert ever since.

Escaping From Adolescence

Roy Fleming was sitting on the couch in his living room in his pajama bottoms watching "The Partridge Family" marathon on TV Land, eating Froot Loops out of the box, and drinking chocolate milk through a silly straw when his phone rang.

"Hello," he mumbled.

"Mr. Fleming?"

"Yaa…"

"Roy Fleming?"

"Uh heh?"

"Mr. Fleming, this is Daniel with Bank & Trust Card Services?"

"Uh-heh?"

"Sir, your account is currently four months past-due…?"

"Right…"

"Wanted to know if you could get your checkbook, we can do a payment right over the phone for you, sir…"

"That's not possible."

"It's not possible? Why is it not possible, Mr. Fleming?"

"Not working…"

"How long have you been out of work, sir?"

"5 months…"

"Really?"

"Uh heh."

"Haven't been able to find a job in 5 months?"

"That's correct…"

"How are you living, then, sir…?"

Roy paused. "That's the trick," he said.

Daniel paused. "Well, Mr. Fleming, you do understand the severity of the situation, don't you?"

"I believe so…"

"Your account will be charged-off in June if you don't clear this matter up, sir…"

No reply.

"Mr. Fleming?"

No reply.

"Mr. Fleming? Are you there, sir?"

Roy sighed.

"Mr. Fleming, why don't you get your checkbook, I can take a check right over the phone, sir-"

"You said that already."

"…Well, sir, it'll cause you a whole lot less aggravation if I could just take a payment from you tonight…"

No reply.

"Mr. Fleming?"

No reply.

"Mr. Fleming, I need a response from you, sir. We have left you numerous messages and you have failed to contact us. Now I can save you a lot of grief, sir, if you'd only-"

"Play ball?" Roy said.

"Sir?"

"I'm depressed…"

"Well, I can certainly understand your…"

"I gotta gun…"

Pause.

"Did you hear me?"

"Yes, sir, I heard you. You said you have a gun."

"Yah and I'm gonna blow my brains out if you don't get off this phone…"

"Well, now, there's no need to do that, Mr. Fleming. Is your checkbook nearby, sir…?"

"YOU ASSHOLE! DID YOU HEAR WHAT I SAID?"
"Sir, there's no need to curse at me or raise your voice. This is a very serious matter. It has escalated to the next level. Now do you want to sit there yelling at me like a maniac or do you want to solve this situation like a mature adult? The choice is up to you… Do you need me to call the police and let them know you've threatened to commit suicide? Because I'll gladly do that for you, Mr. Fleming…"

No reply.

"Mr. Fleming?"

No reply.

"Mr. Fleming, I'll stay on the line as long as it takes, sir. I'm here all night…"

Pause.

"Whaddaya gonna do, sue me?"

"Is that what you want?"

"I don't have deep pockets…"

"Well, I'm sure our legal department will compensate for that, sir…"

Pause.

"What do you say, Mr. Fleming? I know you want these phone calls to stop. I know how annoying they can be…"

"Nobody will hire me…"

"What about McDonald's? I'm sure you could get a job at McDonald's."

No reply.

"Mr. Fleming, you're only making it harder on yourself…"

"SHHHUDDUPPPP!"

"Mr. Fleming?"

"ARGHHHFRUCKKKAVOHH!"

"Sir…"

"FUUUCK OFFFF!"

"Sir, that's very poetic…"

"ASSSHOLLLE!"

"Mr. Fleming, why don't we hang up now and I can call the authorities and have them check you out, make sure you're alright, sir…"

Roy slammed the phone down and unplugged it from the wall.

20 minutes later there was a knock at the door.

Roy looked through the peephole and saw two uniform police officers standing outside. He opened the door.

"Can I help you?" Roy said.

"Sir, is your name Roy Fleming?" the older cop said.

"Yes it is…"

"Is everything alright…?"

"Fine…"

"Do you know why we're here, sir?"

"No, sir, not exactly…"

The younger cop peered into Roy's apartment.

"We got a call from your credit card company. Said you had threatened to commit suicide or something. Do you recall saying anything like that, sir?"

"No, sir. I don't recall saying that…"

"Probably threatened to shoot the guy from the credit card company," the young cop joked and smiled.

"Do you have any weapons?"

"No, I don't believe in them…"

The older cop turned on his flashlight and shined the light it into Roy's place.

"Mind if we take a quick look around, sir, just to see if everything's in order…?"

"Not at all…"

The cops stepped in and were both now shining their cop flashlights.

"Do you have any type of ID on you, Mr. Fleming?"

Roy grabbed his wallet from an end table and handed his driver's license to the younger cop, who copied the license number down in a small notebook.

Meanwhile, the older cop conducted a cursory search of the apartment. He illuminated Roy's bookcase.

"Lenny Bruce, heh?" he said.

"Uh heh,"

"That's alright…"

"You like Lenny Bruce?" Roy said.

"I'm a whole 'nuther person outside of this uniform," and he chuckled.

The younger cop returned the license to Roy.

Satisfied that things were in order, the cops headed for the door.

"Okay, Mr. Fleming," the older cop said. "As I said, we just wanted to make sure you were alright and everything. 'Preciate you cooperating with us…"

"No problem…"

"Sure you're gonna be okay now?"

"Yes, sir, I'll be fine…"

The older cop tipped his hat and he and his partner walked away.

Roy closed the door and went to bed.

Adminisphere

Scene: Two amorphous masses are decompressing at a martini bar, smoking Montecristo Media Noche cigars, drinking dry martinis, engaging in one those conversations that make you go, wtf?

Man A: Uhhh…so who are we targeting again?

Man B: We're targeting somebody who's experienced with that whole measuring, managing, improving and reducing the variability thing and able to identify, target, convert, and onboard mass affluent balance-qualified clients that drive organic growth…

Man A: Mmm. Organic growth. I like that. My Dad used to be an organic gardener.

Man B: And, of course, because this is a high-profile, highly-visible role with an ability to have a significant positive impact on the business, they gotta be able to navigate the matrix and drive collaboration across multiple support-partner organizations…

Man A: Any prospects?

Man B: Jennings in Process Design. He's Black Belt Certified and he knows how to make the complex simple.

Man A: Process Design… what do they do again?

Man B: Basically, decrease risk, manage compliance, reengineering, blah blah blah…

Man A: Huh. Must have missed that day. (Laughs at his joke, and right on cue, Man B joins in. Man B's Blackberry rings. He answers it)

Man B: Hello…Reynolds? His functional business acumen is poor…I don't care if his strategic initiatives achieved breakthrough goals in customer satisfaction, the man is completely ignorant of implementing Six Sigma methodologies to achieve break-through

Hoshin goals. Besides, he's a lousy change agent. And I don't like his PowerPoint presentations.

Man A: (to Man B) Not to mention he has no concept of the risk/reward trade-off and can't even institutionalize error-free quality processes without first consulting a psychic...

Man B: (nodding in response to Man A's comment) ... I don't give a damn if he attends the Oakborough Presbyterian Church! The last time he attempted to extract, measure and analyze data, he wound up in the employee assistance program!

Man A: (Pulls out small recording device, turns it on and speaks into it) Check to see if we can claim a tax credit for Reynolds since his breakdown... (Shuts off recorder, puts it back in pocket)

Man B: Who...? Freddie Mobley?

Man A: Can't work on multiple issues that are in various stages of repair...

Man B: He says he can't work on multiple issues that are in various stages of repair...plus he's a stress puppy...we need a plug-and-play guy, we can't be cockin' around...

(Man A gestures to wrap up the call)

Man B: Gotta go, bro...uh heh...thanks... (Hangs up) Total 404...

Man A: He'll be decruited within the month...

(Their waitress, a sexy young Venus, approaches them)

Waitress: Excuse me, gentlemen? I couldn't help but overhear...I understand you're looking for somebody to skillfully influence broader corporate initiatives while effectively dealing with ambiguity and balancing business unit needs with local portfolio goals...

(Man A looks at Man B; and she suddenly becomes the most

intriguing human being on the earth's surface to them)

Man A: I really think she could improve current processes in order to redirect resources to areas not currently under consideration…

Man B: And she seems to have the kind of vision that is so central to our journey in building a great brand and should be able to make it work in ways it never has before…

Man A: You picked up on that, too?

Man B: Something about the way she took our drink order…

Man A: (To waitress) Gotta resume?

Waitress: I can email it to you…

(They shake hands with the waitress and order two more martinis)

Knowing That The Pain Is His

1

The Dude without a large enough dose of heroin to make him feel like a superhero wonders why his shadow keeps disappearing while he stands in the sun.

There are other things nagging at him this morning, too.

Aching knees, a stiff neck, a hangnail on his thumb, a popcorn hull wedged between his teeth and gums.

It's a long way to rehab from where he's standing, he thinks.

And then his cell phone rings.

"Yo," The Dude says…

"Ready?" says a lazy voice.

"Been ready," The Dude says, his voice already going hoarse.

"Meet me at the Waffle House on the Boulevard in a half hour."

"Okay."

2

The Dude sits down at a booth, orders the All-Star Special Breakfast, coffee, and a glass of water with lemon in it.

The waitress looks like someone he once fucked in the backseat of a Ford Maverick in the '80s.

Marilyn? Jocelyn? Eileen? Marlene?

Something like that.

Too long ago to remember, though.

Just too damn much space and time between that backseat and the booth he's now sitting in.

And he laughs at himself.

3

Charlie finally arrives, looking a little older than the last time The Dude saw him.

"Sorry I'm late, man," Charlie says. "There was an accident…tractor trailer jack-knifed…carrying bananas! 'member that song by Harry Chapin? '30,000 Pounds of Bananas?' That's what it reminded me of…I was like, whaaa? …whuja order, looks good."

"All-Star Special Breakfast."

"I'll do the same."

The waitress comes over.

"Sir, can I get you something?"

Charlie points to The Dude's plate. "Gimme some of that and some coffee."

"Yes, sir," and off she goes.

"So ya awright? All is well?" Charlie says.

"I'm here."

"We're all here, bro. One big happy fucken family."

Charlie looks around, sees who's there. "I gotta win the lottery soon, man…gotta get up on outta here."

"Uh heh."

Charlie shakes his head, nervously drums on the table with his fingers.

"So whucha been up to?" Charlie says.

"The usual."

"Man of action, arncha?"

The Dude shrugs. "It's my life…"

"I feel ya."

The waitress brings Charlie's coffee.

"How long you been workin' here, darlin'?" Charlie says to the waitress.

"About two years."

"Ya like it?"

"Pretty much."

"Got any dreams?"

The waitress looks at Charlie like he doesn't have the right to be asking her a question like that and says, "Doesn't everybody?"

"You gotta point there," Charlie says, and the waitress sort of smiles and asks Charlie if there's anything else she can get him and Charlie says, "No thanks," and the waitress walks back to the kitchen, probably thinking Charlie's crazy or something.

"Certainly have a way with the ladies," The Dude says.

Charlie sips his coffee. "She wasn't my type, anyway."

4

Charlie finishes his breakfast, refuses another refill of coffee, then reaches into his pocket and hands The Dude an envelope.

The Dude reaches into his pocket and hands Charlie some cash.

"Always a pleasure," Charlie says.

"Good luck on the Lotto."

"It's up to five hundred thousand."

"Wow."

Charlie shrugs. "You have your addiction, I have mine."

5

The Dude goes back to his apartment on the west side, snorts some heroin, listens to Pink Floyd's *The Wall,* and suddenly remembers it's Halloween.

"Used to love Halloween," he says, and he goes to the video store to rent "It's the Great Pumpkin, Charlie Brown," but the clerk behind the counter says "Don't have any copies left, man; they're all out…it's Halloween."

"Shit," The Dude says…

"I got Disney's 'The Legend of Sleepy Hollow'," the clerk says…

"Not the same," says The Dude, and he leaves.

6

Feel like a drink, The Dude thinks, so he walks into a bar not too far from the video store, sits down at the counter and orders a gin gimlet…

There are worse places to be, he thinks, and then he begins to list some of them...

Jail...
The hospital...
The morgue...

He can't think of any other places to add right now, but that's okay.

Those seem to be The Big Three, anyway, as far as he's concerned.

The Dude's drink arrives, he thanks the barkeep.

"Normally this slow on Halloween?" The Dude says.

"Pretty much," says the barkeep, and he walks to the end of the bar to ask the man with dark skin and bushy eyebrows if he wants another Woodford Reserve, neat.

7

The Dude finishes his third gin gimlet, pays the tab, wanders outside.

Notices a funny smell in the air.

Mildew combined with something else; pesticides, rotten eggs, sewage.

Can't really tell.

"Weird," he mutters, and then pulling his coat collar up around his ears, The Dude heads west, toward the harbor.

His cell phone rings.

"Yo," The Dude says...

"Dude."

"Yaa."

"I gotta talk to ya, man."

"Who's this?"

"Randy"   He's practically hyperventilating…

"What's up?"

"Man, I want a drink so bad… I'm goin' through some real shit…
I'm stressin' out…you know I lost my job…now it looks like the
bank's gonna foreclose on me…" He groans. "I'm tryin', man, i'm
tryin', it's not easy."

"You can do it, it's in you."

"I'm gonna end up in a fuckin' shelter, man."

"Better there than dead."

"How did you do it, man? How do you do it?"

"One minute at a time… one hour at a time."

"Wowhhh…"

"Kick its ass, man. It's your choice…"

"Lissen – if i slip…"

"You're not gonna slip."

"If I slip, I'm sorry…"

"You're not gonna…"

"Just want you to know, you're the best fuckin' sponsor I ever had, I
just want you to know that."

"You're gonna be alright."

"'Snot the worst thing in the world, though? If I slip? I can still do a do-over, right?"

"You're not gonna slip… stay strong…change your focus… go for a jog, somethin', just keep it movin'."

Randy's breath slows down. "Holy Christ!" Pause. "You there?"

"I'm here"

"I'm tired, man… so freakin' tired."

"You're alright."

"Thanks for being there."

"No problem."

Pause.

"Yeah, lemme go joggin' or somethin'," Randy says. "Take my mind off this shit… thanks, Dude."

"Call me anytime."

"Thanks."

As The Dude hangs up, a female voice calls out to him…

"Hey, baby, you doin' alright tonight?"

The Dude immediately unfolds his phone, dials a number.

"Yo, Charlie."

"Wassup?"

"I need you to talk me down, man."

"What's goin' on? Another hooker?"

"Yeah."

"Ok, just relax. Change your focus, man, you can do it, it's in you. One minute at a time, one hour at a time, you got it, the choice is yours, just keep it movin'…"

I Feel Like I Can't Remember How I Feel

So now that I've finally found my voice, I can begin to write that Marginal American Novel.

I think its major theme will be The Search for Personal Identity.

Because, quite frankly, I still haven't figured out who the hell I am.

So in addition to its being the Marginal American Novel, it'll also be therapy for me.

Because I sure as hell can't afford a therapist.

Besides, I already know what a therapist would tell me if I went to one.

They would tell me I'm still a child and I'm still not ready for adulthood.

There, I diagnosed myself. I'm cured!

So anyway, my protagonist [Okay, you might as well say it's me] is on this search for personal identity. He strikes out into The World alone. Tries to break from society's conventions. Grapples with the notions of loss of personal control and whether people can change their situations in life or whether they are in the grips of forces beyond their control, blah blah blah…

What do I know? I've never written a novel before.

But I have read a few here and there. Every now and then. Whenever the spirit or martinis moves me.

I especially like novels that don't have a lot of big words in them or sound like they were written a hundred years ago by some highly-educated over-achieving European aristocrat.

Okay, so I'm shallow. Sue me.

The point is, my novel's not going to have a lot of words.

I know most novels are like at least a couple hundred pages long, but, man, I just don't have the time to be writing that many words. I'm working a full-time job and I only have a couple hours a night to work on the damn thing. By nine o'clock, I'm ready for bed.

So you can see my dilemma.

And on top of that, I'm going to be forty-five years old in December, so I'm not exactly a wunderkind. Of course, I'm not exactly a wundermensch, either. In fact, there's hardly anything wunder about me at all. And that's not an easy thing for a guy like me to admit. It's bad enough you got me to admit that I don't know who the hell I am.

Like it's a crime to be forty-five and not know who you are.

Do you know who you are?

You don't even look like you know where you are.

Me, I'm in a six-hundred square foot subsidized apartment with leaky faucets and a family of mice living inside my bedroom closet wall.

Nice, heh?

And I keep getting these goddamn bug bites on my legs and arms. I don't know if they're mosquitos or spiders or bedbugs, but they're really pissing me off!

So, as you can see, I have a hell of a lot of obstacles that are getting in the way of me writing the Marginal American Novel; which at this point is probably going to end up being the Marginal American Novella or Short Story or Poem. Or whatever's shorter than a poem.

A slogan maybe?

Can you write about somebody who's searching for personal identity in the form of a slogan?

Oh yah, Nike did it, didn't they? "Just Do It."

Okay, well, there's always variations on a theme.

Every writer steals from every other writer. Shakespeare stole from the Greeks. George Harrison stole from the Chiffons. Milton Berle stole from Bob Hope.

Me, I think I'll steal from Moses.

Hey, it's the greatest story ever told, right?

Better I should steal from Moses than from say the writers of "Hello, Larry."

I mean I would at least like a shot at being reviewed by somebody at the New York Times. I don't care if it's the obituary writer, for Chrissakes, I'm not choosey.

I just gotta come up with a plot now.

I mean, I sort of kind of have a plot.

I just have to figure out how to resolve my inner conflicts.

Errr, I mean my protagonist's inner conflicts.

Which are…

I'm glad you asked.

Somebody once told me there's like anywhere from one to thirty-six plots in all of literature.

I have absolutely no idea what they are. I'll let you go on Wikipedia to find that out.

But because the major theme of my novel is The Search for Personal Identity, I just have to find out my identity. I mean, my protagonist's identity. And then I'll have my novel.

Apparently, there's like a beginning, a middle, and an end to every story, so…

I just have to find the…

Whaddaya they call it?

Structure?

I think that's what they call it.

I don't want you to think this is easy for me. It's not. At all. I mean, quite frankly, I usually get migranes and boils on my ass from trying to be creative..

I don't even think Hemingway got migranes or boils on his ass when he was trying to be creative.

But I do.

Not that that makes me a better writer than Hemingway. God knows I'm not. I'm just saying…

I don't know what I'm saying… probably because I'm drunk… but so was Hemingway.

Some of the time. I don't want any law suits.

Besides, I have no money. I'm a parking lot attendant.

I know it's not the most glamorous job in the world, but it's better than my last job. I was a janitor at a porno theater.

Talk about a self-esteem buster.

Not that it fills me with confidence to be sitting inside a tiny booth calculating parking charges and collecting fees from customers, but, it's a hell of a lot better than mopping up dried semen.

And it gives me a lot of time to think about my novel.

Which I'm sure I'll start any day now.

A Kink Inside

We all had our hands in our pockets and
our heads down.
The Messiah,
who was clearly drunk,
reached into the inside pocket of his long,
black coat, and pulled out a pocket-sized
bible and a flask.
He took a pull from the flask and
looked at us with his one good eye;
he'd lost the other one in a particularly
intense poker game.
"You guys, really, are pathetic," he said.

"Where's your goddamn self-respect?
You look like a buncha school kids,
for chrissakes! Snap the fuck out of it!"
He asked a short, fat man for a smoke,

but the short, fat man said he didn't smoke.
The Big Guy was furious.

"WHADDAYA MEAN YOU DON'T SMOKE?
WHAT THE HELL'S THAT SUPPOSED TO MEAN?
WHY DON'T YOU START SMOKING?
THAT WOULD SEEM TO BE THE LOGICAL THING.
YA GOT SOMETHING AGAINST SMOKING?"

Suddenly, the short, fat man bolted.

The Big Guy shook his head, and spoke softly.

"That's what's wrong with humanity…
everybody's so Goddamn afraid of defending their values!
Now one of you fuckers gotta have a cigarette. . ."

A half dozen of us pulled out smokes and
offered them to the Big Guy,

but he just stared numbly at us.

"Thanks, but I just quit," he said,
opening the holy scriptures.

"In the beginning God created the
heaven and the earth," he said, pausing.
He took another pull from the flask and muttered,
"interesting," and continued reading.
"and the earth was waste and void; and darkness was
upon the face of the deep.
And the spirit of god moved upon the face of the waters."

He paused and looked at us.

"For a hundred thousand dollars. . .
what is the next line? Anybody!"

No one knew.

Not even the seminary student.

The Big Man shook his head violently and screamed,

"AND GOD SAID, LET THERE BE LIGHT;
AND THERE WAS LIGHT!"

The Big Man's face glistened with saliva and
sweat and he began panting and hyperventilating.

We were all getting nervous.

We didn't know what to do, how to react.
We fidgeted in our third-hand clothes,
desperately in need of nicotine and a stiff drink.
The Big Man coughed and spit up some blood.

"Whaddaya, all think this here's a myth,
a legend, a ghost story? Is that what ya'll think?"

Another protracted pause.

"Do ya'll know what freedom is?
What it means to be free? Knowing that when
you die, you'll be old and full of days?
Do you know what the statement means?"
We all looked at him dumbly.

Even the Rhodes Scholar.

"Look, if ya'll aren't I down with this,"
said The Big Guy.
"that's your problem!
Guess I had higher expectations of you. . .
Apparently, it's become more of a
co-dependent issue rather than an
I love you issue. . ."

The Big man cocked his head and smirked.

"Don't say I didn't try. . ."

Our dry eyes quickly disappeared and we
declined to comment.

Say What

It seems that much of what has been said is just said again and again
because someone didn't like the way it was said the first time around,
so they had to say it the way they thought it should have been said.

Besides, people die, they forget, they fall asleep, they go into comas,
they don't read, they stop believing, they no longer pay attention, so it
makes it easy to say something even though it's been said a Billion
and a half times before.

Even what I just said
has been said before
and I'm sure whoever said it first or last,
said it even better than I just said it.

In fact, you're probably saying to yourself right now,
"I could have said that,"
and I'd say you're right,
you could have said it.

You probably have said it.

You may have even said what I said
and said it on your blog and
now other people are saying to themselves
"I could have said that,"
just like you said it to me.

So the next time somebody says something
and you're thinking nobody's ever said
anything like that before, just say to yourself,
"Well it sounds like he's said all he's going to say
and now that that's all said and done, 'nuff said."

Now I Know Where Home Is

Remember getting the message from Pops.

"She's gone," is all he said, and then he broke down.

I told him I'd be there as soon as I could and hung up.

Sat there,
lit another herbal cig,
drank another cup of coffee.
wondered if I was gonna be able to face my remaining family.

Got in my car.

Drove to the hospital.

The Black Crowes "She Talks to Angels" was playing on the radio.

No tears.

No prayers.

No bad thoughts.

Just rush hour traffic and an annoying rain.

Drove into the parking lot of the hospital.

"Son' wanna go in," I said.

But I did.

The nurse said, "Do you want to go in and see her?"

After what seemed like ten minutes, I finally said, "OK," and went in.

As I entered the room, overheard somebody saying, "Her fluids have been drained."

She was lying on her back.

I just stood there.

Saying nothing.

No tears.

No prayers.

No bad thoughts.

Just my tired self.

Had only slept three hours the night before.

Somewhere in my mind I thought about wandering through her garden.

Saw a hot air balloon taking off in the distance.

The sky was gray.

But her roses were in full bloom.

For Some Of Us, We Had To Fight Our Way Out Of A Hole Just To See Some Sort Of Daylight

I recall 1977.

I wore Buster Brown shoes and was expelled for throwing snow balls at a school bus.

I was called into the principal's office so many times that year, it appeared my ass had made a permanent imprint on The Chair.

We called it The Chair for obvious reasons.

We insubordinates liked to fancy ourselves as inmates on death row.

One day I got busted for smoking.

Mrs. Hooper caught me.

It doesn't matter how I got caught.

Or what happened once I was called into the principal's office.

Fact is, I did my penance and got out of sixth grade with most of my balls still intact.

The following year I was in junior high.

Sure, I was a loner.

But I was a loner with people-skills.

I wasn't what you'd call "goal-orientate" or a "go-getter", but I knew how to "work a room" and how to experience those "extremes of emotions."
I was thirteen.

Smoked a half-pack of Camel Lights a day, drank six cups of coffee-milk before lunch.

I was a true one-sixteenth of a bad-ass.

The following year, my parents didn't know whether to send me to private school or military school.

So they compromised and sent me to Catholic school.

Her DNA Is Style

Bijou's mascara runs into her worry lines, making her look even more worried than she's ever looked before.

Has beautiful almond shaped eyes, very sort of pretty feline features, dark hair and light eyes and that's always a beautiful mix, and that ethnic ambiguity: you can't tell if she's Native American, Indian, Caucasian, or Black.

She's a quadruple threat: not only is she hot and has a great walk but she's bi.

She openly flaunted a lesbian affair with a sexy, androgynous, all-American California babe with chick nails & a mega-watt smile.

Her only gripe with men is that she keeps having the same conversation with them over and over again and if she ever gets three Rock Star 21's in her, she'll usually admit to being tired of meeting people because they remind her of the ones she already knows.

When she's lonely, she watches children's faces.

When it rains she burns incense and plays a peyote drum.

Last year she did all her Christmas shopping at a gun and pawn shop, the year before at the Salvation Army and the year before that at the dollar store.

While in junior college, she wrote a short story for her Writing as Communications class entitled, "Stupor, Rigidity, Muteness, & Bizarre or Purposeless Activity."

It began: "He projected enough narcissistic magnetism to pull me in for an ill-advised one-night stand," and ended with, "But I'm not real sure there was enough substance there to constitute a long-term relationship."

She got an A+.

And she hadn't even slept with her professor.

Vitamins For Shaky Fingers

I was writing carelessly, forgetting all I'd learned from "Elements of Style."

Wrote a short story about thugs that were drunk on luck and home-made dandelion wine who had replaced their egos with a statue of the Buddha that began:

"I was experiencing glandular swelling. Wore a pompadour and a poncho in those days. Very few people befriended me. Mighta been cuz I was still sucking my thumb at the age of twenty-seven."

It wasn't Tolstoy, but at least I spelled everything correctly.

The critics said it was schtick.

I got carpal tunnel from writing that fucking story! How could it be schtick?

When my girlfriend read it, she was sure I had based the female protagonist on her.

"This woman wears a caftan," I said. "You don't even own a caftan."

The next day there was a message from her on my answering machine:

"You know how essentially fragile my psyche is…it just doesn't look good, it doesn't feel good. So anyway, experiment, explore, play the field, enjoy."

I was knocked down, upset, unfastened.

I shouldn't have stopped writing, but I did.
Couldn't find my theme, my voice.

My form disconnected, my content deformed.

I dropped to my knees and started to dream.

Somebody was crying.

Somebody else was yelling.

I was driving a black Chevy Impala and no longer felt like an early spring flower.

That's when I realized that it was called a Complex.

In other words I was getting all crossed-up.

That a vertical line sometimes stands for continuous ecstatic love.

A horizontal line sometimes indicates a temporal process.

And that it takes an eternity to make me despair.

Harnessing The Disenchantment

Sitting on the edge of my bed at three o'clock in the morning, rubbing my face anxiously, smoking a cigarette, thinking about that conversation I had with T the other night.

T: "They warned me about getting involved with a poet."

Me: "Who's they?"

T: "My friends. My family. Strangers I'd meet on the subway."

Me: "You told strangers on the subway I was a poet?"

T: "Only when they'd ask."

Me: "Which was how often?"

T: "Every time I brought it up."

Me: "Which was pretty much every time you sat or stood next to a stranger on the subway."

T: [beat or two] "Pretty much."

Me: "And how would this conversation typically unfold?"

T: "I'd start talking about you, what a fabulous, talented guy you are, and they'd ask me what you did for a living and I'd tell them you're a poet."

Me: "Which, I'm assuming always went over really well."

T: "Some take it in stride. Others are, like, he's a what? Who cares? It's my choice. I love you. I think the fact that you're a poet is sexy. It makes me moist."

Me: "Moist like Duncan Hines."

T: "Moist like a porn star."

Me: "So what did these strangers say after you told them i was a poet?"

T: "The usual. You're broke, you're hyper sensitive, too dramatic, living too much in your head, afraid of the Real World, hiding from Reality, suicide."

Me: "Suicide?"

T: [dismissive] "Ya'll are supposed to be suicidal or something, I don't know. You know how people are."

I go to the typewriter, finger the home row keys, type:

"Shaven-headed hipster with his middle finger hovering on the self-destruction button, sees many problems, rolls his eyes.

I open a book of inaccessible poetry and read.

'Yeah so what if I drank away my success and contracted alcoholic hepatitis and I have problems with intimacy and I appropriate words from Samuel Fuller, old blues songs, and the Torah, so what if I'm fragile and vanquished or I'm bored and stoned or I've developed hostile feelings toward my parents and the world or I react to my life with a shrug of the shoulders and a smirk or I'm wandering through a landscape where idealistic young troubadours, struggling to retain relevance and hoping to remake the world, whisper Happiness is Love to disenfranchised urbanites who disappear into the noise of the city.'"

I light another cigarette, pour another drink.

As I've aged, I've started to recycle myself, I think, and I leave my typewriter at quarter after four in the morning, lie down, recall a quote on T's Facebook page.

"Sometimes we need to stop analyzing the past, stop planning the future, stop deciding with our minds what we want our hearts to feel, sometimes we just have to go with…. whatever happens – happens…"

When I finally fall asleep, the blue hour arrives, pouring into my eyes, and I dream, once again, of trying to master the art of the telling detail.

My First Impression Was, How Much Bleach She Uses For That Hair

She kept going on and on about how she'd recently become a vegan.

"Froot Loops are actually vegan," she said.

"Really?" I said.

"Mm hm. Basically, I became a vegan because eating meat and dairy products means animal suffering and slaughtering. I don't want to be a part of that. Plus I gave up meat in support of world hunger."

I nodded.

"At the moment I'm hunting for non-leather shoes because I've only got two pairs. My main concern is my family and friends and acquaintances. Someone always brings up the subject of me being a vegan…and, of course, they don't understand the difference between being a vegetarian and a vegan, so I'm just A Vegetarian." She shrugged bitterly. "And then there's the whole issue about organic foods and how outrageously expensive they are…now, the issue of paying ridiculously high prices for organic fruits and vegetables really pisses me off. Why should I have to pay not to be poisoned? Shouldn't it be the standard that there isn't any crap in my food? I think it's sick. In the same vein: Why should I have to be exposed to pollution and toxic air? Why is that acceptable?"

She looked at me as if I was about to cut the throat of a calf.

That's when her cell phone rang, thank God.

"Ooops, sorry, gotta take this call," she said.

I smiled wearily, and walked toward the exit sign.

Before I reached the doorway, I looked back at her.

She was lighting a cigarette. I wondered if they were vegan cigarettes.

"Dump him!" she said into the phone. "He's got a personality disorder! Leave him at once and go to a local shelter!"

As I got into my car and drove away, I turned on the radio. Dr. Ginger was on. She was a nationally-syndicated talk show host who'd bailed on her own marriage after "discovering her own true brutal nature" and had become somewhat of a heroine among sexually-frustrated, pre-menopausal secular humanists.

"At this point," she was saying to a caller from Santa Cruz. "You should befriend a closeted homosexual who is about your age and needs a 'front'. Trot him around to all the family get-togethers. Tell your parents that you dumped the other guy. You may eventually have to marry the gay guy to keep it all believable, but that's ok – - until you end up sharing a man, but we won't get into that…"

I changed the station, driving away from the sun.

There Are No Rules On When Someone Moves On And Why

They had both married late in life.

She was forty-one, he was forty-two.

Both suffered from chronic depression. Both shared the same cocktail of medications and dosages.

Harry always said he didn't know which was worse; being involved with somebody who was just as miserable as him or being the only miserable one in the relationship.

At least with Claire, he never had to worry about her telling him to just "get over it," or some asinine thing like that. There would be no suggestions of him taking up tennis or joining some bang-the-drums-in-the-woods support group. And she definitely wouldn't be praying for his soul or asking him to accept the baby Jesus as his personal savior. Both were Atheists.

They hadn't even been married a year when Harry returned from a business trip to find Claire wasn't waiting for him at the airport to pick him up as she had planned.

He tried to call her, first on her cell phone, then at home, but there was no answer at either number. After waiting over an hour, he decided she had forgotten about him, so he hailed a cab and told the driver to stop off at the nearest liquor store, where he picked up a fifth of whiskey before heading home.

When he reached the house, it was empty. Claire was gone. He went into the bedroom and saw a DVD on the bed with a note attached. "Watch this," it said.

Harry inserted the disc into the DVD drive and pushed play.

Suddenly he was staring at a tight close-up of Claire's face, her tearful eyes boring right through him. "Harry, I'm very scared," she said.

"But I just look at it like it's the price I have to pay…there's just too much havoc…it's too much…I try not to look back because it's been a…" She stopped herself for a moment, then continued several seconds later. "…very emotional roller coaster of a ride so far…and what really bothers me is that I'm not resilient enough to…survive….well, that's a little strong… I feel like I'm free falling… it's terrifying…God, I've had so many tests and trials…you just don't even realize the moment you're living in…until you sort of look back and…when you're living your life for someone else, you're not living…if you're not true to yourself, you're not true to anyone…I guess you kind of know where I'm going with this…"

Harry paused the DVD, freeze-framing Claire's face, and studied it closely.

It had been such a nice face up until then.

Her eyes looked fatigued, the folds and creases in her skin seemed deeper. And strange how he'd never noticed that droop under her left eye before. Or had freeze-framing the picture caused her face to distort like that?

He pressed the play button.

Claire was now looking down, but the droop was still there. She was reaching for something. Her cigarettes. She lit a Merit Ultra-Light, puffing on it nervously and letting the ashes drop in her lap. Her eyes remained low. "Shit, Harry, I don't know…"

Harry stopped the DVD. "So if you don't know, how should I…?" he said.

Harry got up and went to the bathroom and washed his face. He wondered how other guys would have reacted to seeing their wives asking them for a divorce like that? Electronically. They probably would have been throwing and breaking things around the house by now and shoving their fists through walls and sustaining concussions from banging their lunkheads against concrete surfaces.

He wondered why he wasn't doing any of that stuff. Why he was so calm, as he gazed into the mirror and inspected his teeth?

Just Another Flawed, Byronic Hero

When I was in junior high, my parents made an appointment for me to see the school psychologist because I wasn't performing up to their expectations. I hadn't been "applying" myself.

That was only because I was so friggin' bored.

But of course they didn't wanna hear any of that crap.

So I walked into the psychologist's office, who was this very nerdy sort of stuffy, humorless guy, and I must have sat there for about five minutes before he even acknowledged me; he was so engrossed in whatever the hell he was reading or writing.

Finally he looked up at me over the tops of his glasses because they were sliding halfway down his nose, and without even trying to establish any kind of rapport whatsoever, he said very morosely, "do we have a problem here?"

And being the total wiseass that I was when I was fourteen, I said, "puberty's a bitch, but other than that, life's peachy."

He was not amused.

I didn't care.

I wanted to piss him off; I didn't wanna be there, anyway.

So after a litany of ridiculous questions, to which I answered "don' know" to about ninety-nine percent of them, the good doctor finally came to the conclusion that I was an "underachiever." I lacked "motivation," "direction," "focus." he suggested I might want to consider changing my circle of friends because they might be having a "negative influence" on me. Perhaps I needed to be in the company of more "positive children."

Now…when you're fourteen and an adult refers to you and your peers as "children," you get a little defensive.

I thought to myself, ooh-kay, now it's time to really make a nuisance of myself.

So I took out a pack of cigarettes and tamped it against my hand and pulled out a butt and put it between my lips and he was just very calmly and casually watching me and I lit the cigarette and took a really long drag on it and blew a huge puff of smoke in his face and the man didn't flinch, didn't cough, didn't wheeze, didn't even blink; he was just his usual deadpan, monotonous self.

After all, this was all just in the interest of science to him. he was observing me for clinical purposes and wanted to find out what made me tick. Naturally, he was going to reserve judgment.

So we sat there, not saying anything, completely poker-faced for several minutes and i was just puffing away, having a good old time, and the good doctor, god love him, he was trying so hard to find an opening so he could begin chiseling into my psyche.

He suggested I might have some hostility toward "authority figures" and "the rules of the game."

No shit, Sigmund Freud, for that brilliant insight into a fourteen year old punk who's been blowing smoke in your face for the past five-minutes.

And I had thought I was being so subtle.

Of course, now I can look back on those days and laugh.

Till I cry.

Hell, I'm not bitter.

C'est la vie and all that bullshit.

But the thing that really pissed me off was that moron narced on me for smoking in his office and I ended up getting suspended for three days.

You Can See The True Timbre Of A Person When They Lose

He has no wife, no kids, no girlfriend, not even a girlfriend to rent for an hour or two; just his imagination and lack of social maturity.

Wakes around 6, grumbles, "Don't wanna go to work, mama."

Showers, shaves, dresses, drives to Dunkin Donuts, orders a medium coffee with cream, turns right out of the parking lot, merges left, heads west, inserts Shostakovich's Fifth Symphony into the CD player.

I now know why so many men drink, he thinks.

Because there's another man inside of them.

While at work, he sighs, mutters, "I'm tired," listens to coworkers tell him, "you're just burned-out…"

Leaves at 4:30, goes to the Y, runs on a treadmill for 30 minutes, sits in the steam room, listens to a dislocated soul telling a story of being on the outside, looking in.

"It was one of those very awkward moments. We're all sitting there and somebody wanted to pray before the meal and it was the Lord's Prayer and I was thinking, 'okay, what do I do now?'"

"Always follow your heart," says the guy next to him. "According to God's footsteps."

Drives home, drinks Grand Marnier, smokes a Macanudo cigar, reads the newspaper, watches the local news, eats a bowl of cereal for dinner, reads a novel about a troubled writer who pays the price of honesty, goes to bed.

Lies awake in the middle of the night, mumbles on about his indifference, his coldness, of being alone, self-conscious, isolated, living in a blurry gray tunnel.

Wakes around 6, worries about losing his job because his manager thinks he's "unconventional and withdrawn," and doesn't "follow through enough."

Showers, shaves, dresses, drives to Dunkin Donuts, orders a medium coffee with cream, turns right out of the parking lot, merges left, heads west, inserts Shostakovich's Fifth Symphony into the CD player.

I now know why so many men fail, he thinks.

Because so many other men succeed.

Could Be Damn Near Anything

The kids flying their kites in the park told me they'd stopped believing.

When I asked them what had happened to change their minds, they just shrugged their tiny shoulders & broke out the Bazooka bubble gum & shared one more laugh with the adolescents falling from the monkey bars & the jungle gyms.

So I got in my car. Drove home. Drank a beer. Laid down. Closed my eyes.

My breath was shallow. Couldn't keep my eyes closed. Kept seeing the missing tile from the ceiling.

What was wrong? What went wrong?

I was smiling just the other day. Having a drink with a friend. Counting my blessings. Remembering her cute smile. But it still wasn't enough to heal me.

I started crying.

Didn't know why.

Thought it might've had to do with my obsession with exercise or because I was eating too many carbs…

But I think it was because I was losing a piece of myself.

A piece of this, a piece of that.

Before I knew it, the pieces had turned into
fractions of pieces and were finally reduced to their lowest common denominators.

It Doesn't Get Any Easier, Even If You Keep A Straight Face

The Wrong Rev wore a Dacron shirt,
and began the eulogy by kissing a
statue of the Buddha.

"Brothers and sisters," he said.
"The lonely, tragic hoarders and
haters are among us!"

The mourners in the back pews
flicked their Bics and threw their
damn hands up.

That's when I excused myself.

I was a little cranky.

I needed a smoke.

I stood outside by a statue of a menopausal Mary;
she looked fatigued, as if she were In the
Shadow of a Compromise.

There was a shabby but respectable hotel across
the street with undergraduate memories of
ashen-faced blondes in smocked dresses and
tweed blazers, who were cheek-deep in
existential despair and complaining of
"precarious nervous conditions."

There were secrets hidden within those
walls and layers of pain, too.

I considered checking in but was experiencing
Oscillations of Faith.

I finished my smoke, tossed it on the ground,
and stamped it out.

Looking back over my shoulder into the Sanctuary,
(I'd left the door open),
I noticed the Wrong Rev was sweating and
trying to get hold of the dearly departed soul.

"You were but a bubble on a puddle," he said.
"A bubble that spluttered on a puddle."

I'd heard enough.

I walked home, laid down on my bed,
dreamed of delusions of morality,
and didn't crack an eye until
11 o'clock the following morning.

Little Quirky Esoteric Men

I remember these guys wandering around in the early 90s wearing tee shirts that said BIPOLAR IS SEXY.

They'd get up around noon, smoke a bowl or six, nosh on some Cap'N'Crunch, and watch movies on TCM.

"Hey, dawg, that's Claude Rains! 'The Invisible Man!' Whoa! I saw him on an episode of 'Alfred Hitchcock Presents.' He played this pastor who bet his life savings on a race horse in order to finance a new roof for his church. But I can't remember how it ended, man! Isn't that fucked up? My memory's, like, fading terribly lately, I dunno what the fuck's goin' on!"

Then they'd call up their Source, and speak in code.

"Yo, Marco."

"'S'up?"

"Any potten bush on the horizon, brah?"

"Uh heh."

"Half?"

"Right."

"'Preciate it."

"You da man."

"Time?"

"Thirteen hundred."

"Half past."

"I be's here."

"See ya."

"Wouldn't wanna be ya."

"Never tire a that shit, do ya?"

"Not ashamed to say it."

"Quiet."

Then they'd call their "girlfriends."

"Deena."

"Bruce."

"Whadda ya doin'?"

"Ohh, I just bought one a those jack rabbit vibrators. Ohmyfuckinggod, it's so fucking intense!"

"Hey, favor."

"No booty call."

"Come on, now."

"I'm too soar."

"Pretty please? With whipped cream and sprinkles and a cherry on top?"

"I am raw."

"Deena."

"Bruce."

"I haven't had any in like three weeks."

"Poor baby."

"Don't make me hit the streets."

"I'm not makin' you do anything, punk. You have free will. You do things of your own volition and at your own risk."

"Treat me like a damn step child."

"Aren't you?"

"Bitch....I'm Audi."

"I'll invite you to the wedding."

"What wedding?"

"Me and Jack."

"Jack?"

"Jack Rabbit."

"Never replace me."

"You just don't know."

"Peace and Love."

"Viva la Jack! Viva la Jack! God bless Jack!"

Then they'd get in their '72 Chevy Malibu's, drive to 7-11, purchase two 1/4 pound Big Bite Hot Dogs, a Big Gulp Ice Cream Float, and two packs of Swisher Sweets, and always run into somebody they knew from high school or a job they worked at for three or four days, usually guys with names like Tuffy or Bullet or Scooter or Dice, with the conversation typically going something like:

"Hey."

"Hey."

And that would be it.

They'd get back into their cars and insert Uriah Heep's "Live on the King Biscuit Flower Hour" CD into the player and listen to "Easy Living" twenty-seven times, singing along only to the chorus. *"Easy livin' and I've been forgiven/ Since you've taken/ Your place in my heart…"*

They'd travel toward the Red Light District, but get pulled over halfway there by a motorcycle cop for an expired inspection sticker.

"Sir, do you know why I pulled you over?"

"I dunno, probably somethin' havin' to do with meeting your quotas."

"Your inspection sticker's expired."

"Oh really? Yeah, you're right, it has. Sorry."

"I'm 'onna have to write you a ticket."

"Dude, it's only a couple months overdue… I been meaning to get it inspected, but between my work schedule and everything else that's been goin' on… my mom has ovarian cancer… and I just lost my job."

"You just said your work schedule prevented you from…"

"It did, before, you know, I was just let go today… my supervisor fired me for lack of… something or other… performance anxiety some shit, man… personally, I feel I was set up to take a fall, but, anyway."

But they'd get the ticket, anyway, and drive off, forgetting all about the Red Light District, and head back home, where they'd go back to bed, looking like small, unhappy sleeping Buddahs.

Fugitive From Halloween

In the wake
of a fitful death,
with lips cracked
and septum deviated,
she brewed a cup
of tranquilizers and
unlocked a chest
in the attic
containing childhood screams
and adolescent nightmares
and discovered that
when looking into
the human skeleton,
she could only
focus on one
eye at a time.

That's when she
began to believe
in ghosts who
live only on
the blood they love.

Those Mental Lapses That They've Had

(The Kid is sitting at a table in a bar smoking and drinking mash, reminiscing about The Cause and how it used to give him a reason to get up in the morning. "What happened to those days?" he's overheard mumbling. "Jesus, where have they gone?")

(That's when the Old Timer chimes in).

Old Timer:
I'll tell ya where those days have gone, kid. To the dogs. To those capitalist pigs! Those embarrassments of riches! Whose allegiances are only to the bottom line! Those bastards! Our problem is we never had access to the money! The lobbyists! If we knew then what we know now, oh, baby, things wouldda been so much different… but we never got the recognition we deserved…because history is written by the winners and they never go in chronological order…and the losers are forced to slink quietly into the night, like dogs, without even a fucken pot to piss in… (tears well up in his eyes) …now I ask you… what the hell kinda legacy is that? … back in the day, boy, I was relentless, though, wasn't I…? … you remember…always, "I'll fight somebody tonight… who wants to fight me…?" You know how I was back then…pour me another drink, kid… (The Kid pours the Old Timer a drink and he drains it in a single gulp) …but I never lost my faith in The Cause, though, did I…? … never became disillusioned like all the others…no sir, I didn't push it behind me like everybody else… you know. Right? You know… (takes the bottle and pours himself another drink, holds it up in a toast) God bless, kid… (drains it…sets the empty glass down, quietly, more to himself) God bless… (passes out face down on the table)

Kid:
…the problem wasn't access to the money…or the lobbyists, Old Timer… the problem was us…There were no clearly defined roles…too many personality conflicts, too many mopey, unmotivated characters who were just there to advance their own egos…no distinctive voice, not enough chances taken, not enough capitalizing on opportunities, too many minefields and obstacles that we had to

try and get around…it was like a war and having to go through a lotta the same stuff soldiers go through, only we had no battle plan, nobody was really ever in charge… that was the problem…I could see it so clearly… but what can one man do…?… I could only do what I could and no more… (sips his drink, shakes his head) …what started out as an edge of your seat revolution, turned out to be nothing more than just a bunch of drunken bastards pissing into the winds of a hurricane…

Old Timer:
(suddenly coming to, violently slamming his fist on the table) I will not take responsibility for the contamination of our original vision! I wrote that manifesto! My words! But those bastards raped and reshaped my ideas! And rewrote the damn thing until it was totally corrupted and indistinguishable from its original intent and turned it into some sort of fascist, theocratic, revisionist bullshit! … (falls face down on the table again, passed out)

Kid:
… (raising glass in a toast) To the bleak fucking landscape of the American Soul!

Old Timer: (quietly) Amen…

(Black out)

In The Lurid Light

She applies war paint to her face and adjusts
her do-rag in front of a middle-aged man in a Crown Vic,
takes off her kid boxing gloves, walks toward no place to go,
resigns herself to not a whole lot.
It's not really where she wants to be,
but she knows it's where she has to be.

She's gone from fly girl to goodbye girl
in a matter of minutes.

Her tummy's upset.

Her mouth is dry.

No food in the cupboard.

No fridge in the kitchen.

She walks to the cafeteria,
where all the left-overs are served,
orders liver and onions and asks for extra rice,
but the lady behind the counter says,
"That's 75 cents extra."

"Oh well," she says, "No extra rice today.

She sits down in the corner, near the cobwebs,
feels faint, for some reason, maybe cuz of her
high blood pressure and diuretic meds.
Maybe cuz of nothin' in particular.

She's the kiss of purgatory and has been seen
in public on busses, on trains,
(cuz she can't even get a damn car from the salvation army,
the Kidney Foundation or the Goodwill).

Some days she sits in church,

ashamed to admit she doesn't speak in tongues,
watches the pastor through binoculars and prays
for her lesbian sister and crackhead cousin,
who went to Princeton for a couple of semesters.

"Life is precious," she confesses to the pastor
during a more-than-vulnerable moment,
but the pastor doesn't respond to her because
he doesn't have his hearing aid in and
she winds up feeling snubbed and rubbed
the wrong way and is just about to curse the pastor
out when he suddenly drops dead of a massive coronary.

Wow, she thinks, God's got issues.
No angels singing, no bolts of lightning,
no light at the end of the tunnel.
Things happen for a reason, she reasons,
the reason may be a test;
for which there is no time to study,
no bell curve, no retakes and no passing grade.

Rewriting The Myth

It was a lotta "This" and a whole lotta "That" but very little of "This Here".

That's when most folks were awakened by the sight of a cloudburst (because the starburst had called in sick that day) and the poets and the preachers (who were all hung over from speculating and consecrating) were busy contemplating the massacre of the masses and the massaging of Methuselah (whose plastic surgeon had gone face-down on Rodeo Drive) and infiltrating the filtration system with gallons of overheated water around the Galapagos Islands while simultaneously cleansing their wounds with wounded soldiers.

Now you might think the story would end there, but it doesn't, because there are no congressman around to pass any legislation because all the lawyers have been disemboweled by bird shot and the president is limping comfortably through his third scotch and soda, awaiting his tribunal, his escape hatch, his flask, his gasmask of red death, so he can stay on task; if he's not too busy testing us, molesting us, arresting us, investing in somebody else's future (other than our own).

Who's to blame? He's to blame? You're to blame? I'm not to blame. I'm never to blame.

The news reporters, those trod down upon troglodytes, smoking their microphones and breathing in Mexican gas fumes from a pipeline in Alaska, made the story about themselves rather than the Pope, who was busying Herself with such Popely matters as separating the zealots from the hermits and the saints from the forty-niners and then the Prime Minister showed up with her unstoppable rusty iron teeth and blue goodness in her veins, the kind that glowed whenever you showed her a picture of Medusa; she played me like a toy piano, boy, as I was tickling her ovaries, then walked away, without even glimpsing at my collection of collect phone calls and piano wire.

If she was a democrat I might have invested in her ad campaign, but she was an amateur objectivist, (and pro Ayn Rand), and quite inclined to recline next to her feline, which would have created a rift between her and my tweety bird, who sometimes sings in tune, sometimes performs the concerto for fellatio in c-minor on my piano wire, and sometimes watches me relaxing into the evening with a ruthless, toothless beauty queen from Wasilla, Alaska, who's just seventeen and just could not abstain, it was easier to sustain the pregnancy instead of being clean as a thistle, with eyes not unlike misguided missiles.

Which is when I met Cactus Johnny. We were once pals. Till we had a falling apart at the seamstress. And because I had no formal training in the wholesale clothing and apparel industry, we pleaded with our pleated pants not to bunch up around our crotches, even though it was painfully obvious no one would ever mistake those bunches for erections.

That Pale No Hoper

From L.A. I ventured east to NYC where I worked part-time in a photographic lab, enrolled at the School of Visual Arts, majored in didn't apply myself, minored in mind-altering experiences, tried to figure out what was between a major and a minor, thought maybe I'd have some luck there.

Ended up working for (and getting paid weekly) by the Kidney Foundation, who were in need of "friendly, out-going people" to schedule clothing pickups.

"Great supplemental income for stay at home moms and senior citizens," the ad said. "All other welcome to apply."

I figured I fit the category of "all other" like a mousquetaire, which is exactly why Mrs. Therkleson hired me.

"We enjoy young men with beards," she said. "You remind us of our husbands."

Not knowing how to respond, I simply thanked her and told her I'd always been a huge hit with stay at home moms and senior citizens.

She said she initially had some reservations about hiring me because she thought I was "counterculture."

I assured her that my values and lifestyle were in complete congruence with those of the prevailing culture.

"I do enjoy a good sense of humor," she said.

At nights I lived in a YMCA near the United Nations, where I met exchange students from France and Italy and Russia and Sri lanka, Greece and Israel, played pool with prophets, philosophers and scholars from NYU, the New School, and the Pratt Institute, survived on Fruity Pebbles, distilled water, Shiraz, carrots and Baby Ruths.

Met a young woman named Mary, born in Queens, educated at the

Wooster school in Connecticut, Irish Catholic, taller than me, smarter than me, more sheltered than me, lovelier than a spider's web at dawn.

"I want to teach on an Indian reservation," she said.

"Really?"

"Either that or join the Peace Corps."

"Both are noble."

"I also want to write."

"Have you written anything?"

"I wrote a poem the other night. Can I read it to you?"

"Please."

She took out one of those black and white marbled-covered composition notebooks, opened it, and read from it.

"I was standing in the front yard watching my mother. Her hair was tied in a messy knot in the back of her head. A few greasy strands clung to the side of her face. 'There's so much to be done,' she said. I, on the other hand, was waiting for the happy ending I could carry out into the real world. Or at least the good, pacifist man to rewrite the vision of the human community."

She closed the notebook, found my eyes again, said nothing, waited.

I nodded meaningfully, but could not find the words to express my feelings. I swallowed hard, my eyes produced a brilliant gleaming glow.

"Kind of poignant," I said.

"You think so?"

"I'm no critic, but…it definitely found a place in my heart."

She beamed.

Shortly thereafter, she moved to San Francisco to become an investment banker, while I headed south to Miami to work as a bartender in a predominantly black nightclub called the Neo Nubian. There, I was accepted, for some reason. The sistas adored me, the brothas thought I was ai'ight. I dated many black women during that time and found them to be resplendent and resolved. Some prayed for my soul, others just shook their heads and smiled, called me "stoopid," "craazy," and "off the chain."

While I tended bar, I studied for the paramedic licensing exam, the postal exam, the firefighter's exam, the police officer exam, the civil service exam, the telephone company exam, even the armed services vocational aptitude battery, and failed them all.

Then one sunny afternoon, as I was having several dirty martinis with my friend Selina at an outdoor cafe, we were approached by a svelte man in khakis and a white Oxford shirt buttoned all the way up to his Adam's apple.

He said his name was Klein and he was an independent film producer. He'd been watching me from across the street, thought I had the kind of a face which might excite anesthetic admiration, and wanted to know if I'd be interested in doing a walk-on role in a movie he was currently shooting in South Beach.

"Do I get paid?" I said.

"A thousand bucks," he said.

I pointed toward Selina. "What about her?"

Klein looked blankly at Selina. "OK," he said.

Selina and I played a swinging couple trying to pick up another married couple at a parent teacher's association meeting.

I had lines like, "I'm in real estate. I don't know how *real* it is, but I make a comfortable living."

It ended up winning some film festival in the Czech Republic.

I was singled out.

One reviewer called my performance "impregnable."

Another compared me to Leif Garrett.

A Hollywood agent offered to represent me, but I told him I couldn't live with the pressure of being overexposed like that.

So I moved back to the Nutmeg state, where my aptitude for isolation was tremendous, and tried once more in vain to reinvent myself.

My Watery Spunk

My point is…

A very small percentage
of the female population
is even interested in me.

Not that I'm bragging.

The last female
who had the lukewarms
for me was Sheila Shmortzman.

She had eczema on her hands.

"I'm very self-conscious about it,"
she said. "You figure it's the first thing
people see when you shake hands.
The creams don't work.
I'm taking these pills now.
makes schmoozing really challenging."

I told her I didn't even notice.

"You're just being kind," she said.

"No, I'm not," I said. "I've got an astigmatism."

"Yeah?" she said. "I got pangs of
anxiety and nervousness minutely.
top that."

I couldn't.

"Arnchya gonna ask me for my number?" she said.

I blushed. "I'm married," I lied.

She glanced at my ring finger.

"How come you don't wear a ring?"

I wasn't fast enough on my dogs.
I never am. I'm a lousy improviser.
If I was in Second City, I'd need a script.

"I forget," I said.

Her eyebrows arched. "You forget?"

I told her I'd recently undergone
electroshock therapy and it had
temporarily affected my memory.

She believed me.

Believe it or not.

She appeared to want to
delve further into this
but I could tell the editor inside
of her had crossed out her curiosity
with an imaginary red pen,
turned the page and got a paper cut.

"So," she was careful. "You have a few issues?"

I paused,
scratched the itch in my left eye,
pursed my lips, and sniffed some stale oxygen.

"I'm encumbered," I said.

She nodded with social worker compassion.

Fortunately, she didn't challenge me.

I was so grateful.

I get no thrill from being challenged.

Sheila continued to nod.

She's nodding too much, I thought.
Why is she nodding so much?
She should really stop nodding now.
Maybe she has some sort of
muscle spasm that causes her to
nod uncontrollably?

Finally, she stopped nodding.

I was relieved.

"Life is really a test of one's…"
She searched her cerebral data base
for just the right word.
About a minute and a half later she said,
"Yeomanly inclinations."

On cue, I eyed my watch,
which I wasn't even wearing that day.

I lost a thousand cool points immediately.

Choosing To Fill The Role

She came home. Asked me for a cigarette. Told me I'd be sleeping on the couch. When I asked her why, she said, "There is no greater love than a woman and her Wild G-spot Vibrator."

"What the fuck's that sposta mean?" I said.

She just laughed. Refocused on the book she was reading, the journals of John Cheever. "You really oughta read this, honey," she said, inhaling a piece of lemon raspberry cream cheesecake and washing it down with vanilla-flavored soy milk.

"Why?" I said.

"Cuz he's a frightened little child just like you" She cackled like a hyena, wet her index finger, turned the page, then looking at me out of the corner of her eye muttered, "I'm just playin'."

I went upstairs. Passed by the hallway mirror. Looked at my face. Aside from the touch of gray in my nose hairs, I seemed to be aging, if not gracefully, certainly bravely.

I walked into the bedroom. It smelled of vinegar; my lady had recently douched.

I flashed back to the days when I was a smooth, charming, lovable (in my own irascible way) rock and roll slut in a G-string who created subtlety and nuance with just a raised eyebrow or a slight sweep along my bottom lip with my tongue.

That's when I met my lady. She had a cigarette in one hand and a Kallua and something in the other. Caramel colored skin, dark hair, blue blue eyes. Very sexual vibe about her. A real minx. She was just like so there, so perfect.

"I've just spent three months at an inpatient psychiatric program," she said. "The two biggest lessons I learned from all that counseling was that it's hard to compete against people you've developed relationships with and there's a lot of ways to be intimate. It's not all just sex."

As I worked myself into her later that evening, she said, "Charisma I think is very important. Women are all about sexy."

After I came, I rolled off of her, and stared at several small circles of water stains on the ceiling.

"Looks like you gotta roof leak," I said. "Or a condensation problem."

"Well, which is it?" she said.

"Not sure. Musta missed that day in plumbing school."

"Can you fix it?" she said.

"Doubt it."

"Damn, I need to get me one a those mechanically-inclined guys."

I laughed, and fell off to sleep.

As that memory faded, I heard my lady calling for me from downstairs. "Baby, somebody's lighting off firecrackers! Let's go see 'em!"

I looked out the window. A Chevy Impala was backfiring as it charged down the road. "It's not firecrackers," I said. "It's a car backfiring!"

"Well, let's go find some, then!" she said.

I put on my shoes and we left.

It's Not What You Write – It's What You Don't Write

[Bill is called into his manager's office]

Ed Bill, let's get down to brass tacks.

Bill: I've never liked that expression.

Ed: Focus, Bill.

Bill: I'm actively listening.

Ed: But you're not focused.

Bill: My eyes are fine; I just had them checked. Little bit of an astigmatism, but…

Ed: Bill, I came across your blog…

Bill: [this catches his attention] Oh really?

Ed: Yes, I did. And I have to say…

Bill: How did you…

Ed: [waiting as long as he can] How did I come across it?

Bill: Yeah.

Ed: It was sent to me.

Bill: By whom?

Ed: That's confidential.

Bill: Wow, that's unfortunate.

[pause]

Ed: So you're a writer?

Bill: [slight shrug] Of sorts.

Ed It's some strange stuff, man; I really didn't understand any of it… It's very… [searching] What's the word?

Bill: Esoteric?

Ed: Vulgar.

Bill: Vulgar? Really?

Ed: You use a lot of swear words.

Bill: Do I?

Ed: And there's an awful lot of sexual stuff goin' on.

Bill: Mmm.

Ed: It's like a totally different side of you…I wasn't quite prepared for any of that.

Bill: What do you mean, a totally different side of me?

Ed: I mean, at least around *here* you come across as such a quiet and polite and deferential guy...But your *writing*, man...

Bill: What about my writing?

Ed: It's so. Angry and bitter and rebellious.

Bill: You were offended?

Ed: [careful about how he wants to say this] Wouldn't say I was of*fended*… it was just...an eye-opener...

Bill: [nods] Hmm…

Ed: And, obviously, you've put me, *us*, in a rather awkward position.

Bill: How so?

Ed: Well, it's out there. Everybody knows about it. My manager knows about it. His manager knows about it. It doesn't look good. This is some very racy stuff. I was actually blushing at one point…

Bill: You? Were blushing?

Ed: Maybe not "blushing blushing" … but it's some pretty racy stuff. Very radical. Are you a radical?

Bill: I don't know. What is a radical?

Ed: Politically, are you…a leftist?

Bill: If anything I'm a centrist.

Ed: [surprised] Really?

Bill: Yeah, I mean, I don't essentially consider myself a political animal at all, but if I absolutely *had* to choose *some* direction…

Ed: Huh, that surprises me. From your writing, I would not have necessarily classified you as a centrist.

Bill: No?

Ed: Definitely left of center. Like *way* left of center.

Bill: See, I don't even know what those terms mean.

Ed: [in thought, perhaps trying to understand Bill] Well, as I said, this is not exactly easy for me.

Bill: What are you gonna do, write me up? [slight chuckle]

Ed: I'm afraid I'm gonna have to terminate you.

Bill: [surprised] *Terminate* me?

Ed: [a beat or three] Look, if it was up to me…

Bill: Don't gimme that shit if it was up to you! It *is* up to you! Don't try to pass the buck, ed! What's the big deal? A bunch of silly little stories on a silly little blog that nobody even reads. Who ratted on me? Donna?

Ed: I told you, that's…

Bill: Confidential, I know… [shaking his head] Wow, I'm like… [holds up hands in frustration] So, whadda ya, gotta call loss prevention, have me escorted out?

Ed: Actually, I do.

Bill: [hoping it's not so] This is unbelievable. What about all the IM-ing going on around here? The personal emails? The online games? Are you like totally oblivious? Are you not aware…?

Ed: We're aware.

Bill: But me, you're gonna make an example of.

Ed: You got caught.

Bill: Oh, so can I catch somebody? Can I walk through the building and catch my coworkers fuckin' around on their computers and will you fire them, too? [gets up] Come, ed, let's take a walk.

Ed: That's not necessary. [picks up phone, dials extension]

Bill: Tom plays online poker all the time. Come *on*, let's go bust him. Come on!

Ed: Hi, Greg, will you please come to my office and escort Bill Tomlinson out of the building? Thanks.

Bill: Ed, I am not gonna take the fall for this! I'm sorry, man! [leaves the office and begins walking through the hallways searching for coworkers to expose. Comes across an office and knocks on the door]

Voice: [from inside] Yes?

Bill: Shelly, it's Bill.

Boyce: Yes, Bill?

Bill: [knocking frantically] Can I come in?

[the door opens and Shelly stands there bewildered ed]

Shelly: What's going on?

[Greg, from loss prevention, rushes down the hallway toward Bill]

Bill: Tell Greg about all those times you went online to order all that shit from Amazon and QVC, and eBay. Go ahead, tell him!

Shelly: What are you talking about?

Greg: Bill, don't make a scene, man, let's just go quietly, OK?

Bill: [walks across the hall to another office...the door is ajar, so he bursts in... a man, Chris, is sitting at his desk looking at Bill like he's crazy] And, Chris, you are always playin' fantasy football, don't deny it!

Greg: Bill...

Bill: I am not the only one! Janice in accounting, she does all her online banking at work... and Richard in marketing, gets on all these crazy frikkin' fetish sites! Pissing and shitting...how is that turn-on?

Greg: Come on, buddy, let's go...

Bill: Why me, Greg? [almost whimpering] Why am I the fall guy?
Bro, I'm just trying to be a goddamn writer! I'm tired of working! I
wanna write… I just wanna fucking write, Greg… I wanna get
published so I don't have to work anymore… [drops to his knees,
holds onto Greg's leg] I'm tired of working, Greg. Can you
understand that? I'm frikkin' tired. I mean, have you actually sat
down and read any of my stuff? Have you *really* read it? I'm a social
satirist, Greg. There are just so many injustices. So many crazy,
corrupt, unethical, duplicitous, mean, sucky people in this world. I'm
just trying to do my part by exposing them and capturing some of
them on the page and bringing them to light. Can you understand
that? A writer's gotta write just like a… loss prevention guy's gotta…
prevent loss. We're in the same business, Greg. I'm trying to prevent
loss, too. Loss of hope. Loss of faith. Loss of innocence. Loss of
sanity? Don't do it, Greg. Don't give in to these capitalist thugs. 'Cuz
once they've come after me, they're gonna come after you, too. [a
group of Bill's coworkers have now assembled outside Chris' office
and are staring in utter amazement at the scene in front of them…Bill
begins pointing to some of them one by one] And you and you and
you and you… They're gonna come after all of us. And once they've
gotten us, they'll go after somebody else until there's nobody left and
that'll be the end of civilization as we know it. [ed has made his way
through the crowd and is standing over Bill] You see, you can't just
terminate *me*, ed. You gotta terminate everybody here. Because we're
all complicit… we're *all* to blame for *some*thing. We're *all* at fault. Even
you, ed… all those times you went on craigslist. You know what I'm
talking about, don't you? [ed looks at him as if to tell him to shut up]
Casual encounters? m4m? Hmm? [ed shakes his head] That's right,
ladies and gentleman, ed listed an ad. "White bottom dude seeks big
black dude." ed's got a bad case of jungle fever, folks. Or how about
the "nice quiet shy guy with a kinda kinky side looking for horny
versatile twink…" That was a classic, ed. Boy, you think *my* stuff's
racy…

Ed: That's not true.

Bill: Greg, you can investigate stuff like that, right? I mean, you guys
spent god knows how much money on that software that tracks our
keystrokes, right?

Greg: Right…

Bill: [to Ed] So whadda ya say? Mr. White Bottom Dude?

Ed: You're fired, Bill.

Bill: Did ya'll hear that? [mimicking Ed] "You're fired, Bill." Did you hear the absolute hollowness? The cold, distant, unfeeling, uncaring tone of this paunchy, pale, workaday drone? [some giggles from some of Bill's coworkers] This lazy, predictable, petulant, anxiety-racked neurotic? [more giggles]

Ed: [to Greg] Get him out of here…

[Greg grabs Bill and lifts him onto his feet]

Bill: This lonely, clichéd, ambiguous example of middle management dressed in khakis and a Pinpoint Oxford Button-down Collar Dress shirt… [he allows Greg to escort him out, but continues shouting at Ed and the others] Who probably lies in bed, staring at the ceiling, terrified of the void and the existential horror of being alive. A man constantly in search for a place where he can be the chief visionary, the chief strategist. Well, guess what, Ed? There are no happy endings in life. You better get used to that. There is only the indifference of the universe. It is all but a meaningless little flicker.

[and Bill is gone]

Ed: OK, people, back to work…

[the crowd disperses]

[two coworkers, Joy and Ron, walk back to their offices]

Ron: Have you read any of Bill's blog?

Joy: I have.

Ron: What did you think?

Joy: I think his writing has a very arbitrary, abstracted quality. I mean, where's the emotional intensity? The gamble? Where's the performing surgery on himself? Looking as deep as a person can look inside himself. Self-torture as an art form. I didn't see any of that.

Ron: And I don't feel much electricity coming from the page and it's not really providing something only good writing can give you. There's no emotional core. I was looking for a memorable poetic voice. There's absolutely no alliteration, no consonance.

Joy: Exactly…

[Fade to black]

More Poignancy In Moments

Well, I was having trouble writing an ending to whatever the hell it was I was writing at the time, so I grabbed a beer out the fridge, hopped into the old Impala and went to see this "divine personality" named Ranjit to see if I could get unstuck.

Ranjit was one of those "gurus" who promises to unlock your hidden potential so you can achieve all kinds of personal power and shit.

He said, "Close your eyes, open your mind…" Told me I was eating "angry food…" Meat, processed foods, preservatives, blah blah blah. I should be eating "happy foods." Fruits, vegetables.

I said there are Cambodian Buddhists who eat meat. Why are you telling me I shouldn't eat meat?

He said he understood there are some Cambodian Buddhists who eat meat, but you will be a much happier man if you do not eat meat.

I said, do you think I'm an unhappy man?

He smiled and nodded his head.

"What makes you think I'm so unhappy?" I said.

"The mere fact that you asked me if I thought you were unhappy tells me you're unhappy."

I got mad at Ranjit.

Told him he was an intellectual fake and a fraud and a charlatan and I stormed out of there and headed straight for the nearest bar and drank until I was drunk and passed out in the men's room and was escorted out by an undercover copper who told me to get my ass home or he'd arrest me for disorderly conduct and do you know I almost slugged him? Almost hit the son of a bitch.

And then I heard this voice in my head. My mother's voice. She said, "Go home. I have cookies waiting for you." And I told the copper that, too.

He looked at me like I was crazy.

Maybe I was.

Maybe I still am.

As I was leaving, I said to the copper, "I'm just one more post adolescent, faux nihilist who's unhappy because he gets drunk, fucks evil, crazy baby mamas, eats meat and processed foods." And the copper looked at me deadpan and said, "That's funny, cuz to me you look exactly like an anti-hero who ventured out on a quest to seek the golden fleece but couldn't kill off any monsters or face any hurdles, so by the time he returned home to knock off his pops and assume the thrown, pffft, the kingdom was gone."

I just looked at the copper, the way I always look at coppers, like I'm looking at the ingredients on a bag of snack chips that are high in trans fats, and said, "Thanks, sounds like I just found an ending to my story," so I went back to my room at the boarding house, locked the door, sat down at my Underwood Universal portable typewriter, and wrote the final paragraph of my story.

"Back then, I was constantly getting faced with my own humanity and the only way I knew how to keep myself from going crazy was to zoom off on a lost weekend of debauchery for the sheer drunken hell of it and pound back the kamikaze shots with women who had despair in their faces that was a mixture of tragedy and comedy; but I'd always end up getting in my own way and feeling ridiculous, so I'd burrow my way back into my emotional shell and pray that one day I'd be redeemed by the love of a pulled-together woman because i knew I had so little time left…"

Well-Couched And Well-Protected

Always the onlooker, always outside,
borrowing laughs and sudden gestures,
the droop of sadness.

People were his food and he ate them up hungrily.
His appetites were large but he was never quite full.

Neither was his suitcase.

He thought sleep was a waste of time and if he slept
he might miss something.

He prowled through the nights like a hunter.

He'd borrow papers,
see what was playing on Forty-second street and
he'd go to three features to stretch out the night.

Sometimes he'd register at a small hotel that was
left behind when glamour moved out of town,
but he found a second home, Jerry's Bar,
where he was always welcome.

His mind went away and hid somewhere.

Pounded the pavement looking for work and
he wrote letters home.

Why do I do these things, he wondered.

And he really didn't know.

Shy, sensitive about people getting too close to him.

Battered By The Elements

She handed me a glass of scotch, and asked me if I wanted a little water in it.

"No," I said .

She lifted the short hairs above her eyes and was about to say something, but censored herself.

I took a sip of the scotch. It tasted better than I'd remembered. and I didn't even wince when I swallowed.

"Where does all this sadness come from?" she said.

I shook my head, took another sip. "Got a lot of memories," I said.

She refilled my drink. "You know, it's all about fresh thinking," she said. "Something better. . ." She paused slightly, and tightened the grip on the tumbler in her hand. "I was in psychotherapy for a year and a half when I was a teenager…and my psychotherapist would always ask me this question whenever I lost my focus. . .which was often. . .How do you get back to the fundamentals of life?. . . and I never knew how to answer that question. . . I was sixteen years old. I'd been rearranging the deck chairs up until that point, what the hell did I know about the Fundamentals of Life?" She sighed. "Then one day, I finally got the balls to say to him, you know, I don't know how the hell to answer that question. I don't have a fucking clue what you're even talking about!. .. . . S.O.B just shrugged and said, 'oh well, then'…Like, hey, no big wup… Guy's making ninety thou a year, 'oh well, then'. No insight, no feedback, no diagnosis…So then my parents sent me to private school after I told them I was having sex. . ."

"Why'd you tell them that?"

"They asked," she said.

I was really beginning to like the woman. She seemed just as confused and conflicted as me. I motioned for a refill.

"Ohh, a professional drinker," she said, pouring me another.

"Professionals earn money," I said. "Drinkers are perpetual amateurs."

She sniggered. "So why are you still single?"

I remained unflappable. "Oh well, then," I said.

She liked that. "You're cute," she said.

Our heads loomed closer and closer until our lips made a cautious link-up. There wasn't much passion in it, but it was still a good kiss. Besides, I hadn't been kissed like that in years, so any kiss would have been a good kiss at that time.

When it was done, we closed our eyes and retightened our lips.

I recalled a passage from a book I'd recently read:

"...it is axiomatic with him that one is insulted
and humiliated at every turn. . .he is used to
physical suffering and the degradation of the
body. . .the background of these characters is
empty. . .are of unexplained social status. . .
often courteous mannerly, especially to ladies. . ."

She sighed, "Don't feel sorry for me, even though I'm not in love. It's my problem..."

That's when we fell asleep.

Looking More And More Threadbare

I

Well, I was trying to stay on my hustle by working for this company that paid me to hold up a sign on the side of the road: "Store Closing! Liquidation sale! 50% off everything! Everything must go!" when my cell rang.

It was my supervisor.

He told me the company was moving in a different direction and I was not going to be a part of it.

"Different direction," I said. "The store is going out of business…"

"You'll get your final check in the mail…"

"But, dude, why are you firing me? Am I not connecting with motorists? …I know, I make too much money, right?"

He hung up.

II

Unfortunately, I ran out of my eligibility for unemployment benefits, having exhausted both the standard 26-week eligibility period and a 13-week extension, so I submitted a resume over the internet and a recruiter called me from Florida and explained, in excruciating detail, the job duties associated with the position as well as the company's mission statement and how it was structured. "Does it sound like something you'd be interested in…?" he said.

"Yes," I said. "Absolutely…"

So he scheduled an interview for me the next day and I had to borrow my girlfriend's car to go to it because it was ninety-three degrees and my car had no air conditioning.

III

While I waited in the lobby for my interviewer, two security guards were commiserating about another employee.

"The dude is so paranoid…"

"Totally paranoid…"

"Everyone's out to get him…"

"And I thought I had trust issues…"

"You know he got written up the other day for too many tardies…"

"It's that heffer he's messin' around with…"

A cell phone rang. It belonged to the one who made the comment about the heffer. She answered it and immediately began arguing with the caller about the laundry not being done. The conversation became so contentious that the other security guard had to tap her on the shoulder and ask her to take the call outside.

As the security guard walked toward the door, she said, "I don't care if you have all the clean clothes you need for the week…you are the laziest piece of shit I have ever known…if you would just put down that goddamn remote and take ten minutes to…"

IV

Ten minutes later I was greeted by two young women who escorted me into a tiny conference room where they proceeded to ask me questions like:

"What frustrates you on the job?"

"What education and experience do you bring to this position?"

"Describe a time when you helped your team achieve a goal."

Neither one of them made eye contact with me as I answered their questions; instead, they were both feverishly writing down everything I said and waiting for me to finish completing my answers so they could ask me the next question from the form.

When the interview concluded, my tie was off before I reached my girlfriend's car.

V

The next day, the recruiter called, offering me the position.

"It pays twenty thousand dollars," and he began parsing the benefits package. "Any questions so far…?"

That's less than I make now, I thought. That sucks. "Is there any wiggle room as far as the salary is concerned…?"

The recruiter paused. "Uhh… there very well may be some wiggle room… can't say there will be… can't say there won't be… I think there may be some wiggle room… I think… but, of course, that is totally beyond my realm of control… it's a corporate decision…I am merely the messenger…I do want you to understand, though, that this part of the conversation never happened, ok?… Do you read me…?"

"Yessir…"
"It never happened… It was not discussed…What I will need you to do is think about it over the weekend… come back to me Monday, tell me, I decline the offer of twenty thousand, but would like to counter with X… you understand…?"

"I do…"

"I will then take X to my bosses who will in turn either accept your offer of X, or decline it… understand, though, there will not be a second or third round of negotiations… so come prepared on Monday morning to give me your maximum offer…alright?"

"Understand," I say.

VI

Monday morning, I called the recruiter.

"I'm declining the offer of twenty thousand," I said. "But would like to counter with thirty…"

The recruiter giggled. "For this job?"

He had a point.

So I accepted his offer of twenty grand.

I didn't have much choice.

It was either take the job or move in to the men's shelter.

What the hell.

I guess there are worse jobs than being the mascot of a soul food chain restaurant.

The Tyranny Of The Majority

Well, the rent is late
and now I'm joined by
the glowering mice
who feel more entitled
to this apartment
than me.

A Riddle Wrapped In A Mystery Inside An Enigma

The paparazzi gathered around me,
quoting my facial expressions.

I was pleased to see that my furrowed brow
did not make the morning headlines.

However, they completely took my
pursed lips out of context.

And I was not
'staring with brooding, sullen anger,'

Nor was I
'taking sidelong glances or glowering with hostility.'

I was merely experiencing rapid eye blinking and nose scrunching
because I had forgotten to take my facial tic meds.

Assholes.

Forgotten By A Departing Circus, Long Ago

The movie opened with an old clown
sitting on a swing, smoking,
and sipping from a flask.

A young girl approached
him cautiously. Stood in
front of him. Asked him,
"Why are you all by yourself?"

The old clown said,
"It's a long story, kid."

The girl reached into her
pocket, pulled out a Fireball, and
offered it to the clown.

The old clown shook his head.

The girl shrugged, and
walked away.

The old clown shouted at the girl,
"YOU WORTHLESS LITTLE SHIT!"

The movie ended with the
psychiatrist and the priest being
run off the road into the ocean by
the old clown, who'd spent the entire
movie traumatized by the discovery of
a diabolical truth;
science and theology had failed him.

The next day the clown walked
into a lake and became one with something.

The screen faded to black

and the credits rolled.

A Man Running In Orange County

1.

I got up, got dressed, drank some coffee, lit a cigarette.

Walked to the bus stop.

Boarded the crosstown bus.

Sat next to an old woman who smelled like Vicks VapoRub.

She was reading The New Yorker.

Talk of the Town.

Every now and then she'd giggle; but you could tell she was a little self-conscious about giggling in public because she'd quickly look out of the corner of her eye to see if anyone was watching her.

But nobody was watching her.

We were all immersed in our own thoughts and feelings.

Awaiting our arrival to our destinations, our Point B's.

I was on my way to see my therapist.

Somebody suggested I might need one, so I figured what the hell?

There are worse things to spend your money on.

I looked over at the old lady; she'd finished reading *Talk of the Town* and was now flipping pages.

Nothing seemed to interest her. I don't even think she was looking at the titles of the articles.

I think she was just looking for something to do until she reached her stop.

When she came to the last page, the old lady shook her head and sighed. "It's a shame. I spent a dollar seventy-five cents on this and all I read was 'The Talk of the Town.'"

"I did see you giggling a few times, Ma'am," I said. "That's gotta be worth something."

The old lady thought about that and shrugged.

"That's one way to look at it," she said.

"Yes, Ma'am."

"You have an inborn gift for positive thinking."

"It's something in the genes," I said.

"Interesting," she said.

We didn't say anything for the rest of the trip.

There really wasn't anything to say.

I've always had trouble making small talk with strangers, anyway.

I made a mental note to discuss that with my therapist as I deboarded the bus.

2.

My therapist was running late.

"I apologize," she said. "It was domestic in nature."

"No problem."

I waited.

"Well, the floor is yours," she said, impatiently.

I really didn't know where to begin.

And I didn't feel like telling her about my trouble with making small talk with strangers.

Seemed insignificant.

"I'm sorry," I said. "I really don't have much to say today."

"You don't have much to say? Or you choose not to have much to say?"

She had me.

Again.

"Can't fool you, can I?" I said. And then I felt ashamed for saying something so inane.

"It's not about not fooling me," my therapist said. "It's about not fooling yourself. I've said this repeatedly."

That was her subtle little way of hitting me upside my head.

"However, if you really don't have anything to say..." she said.

I cleared my throat. "Well, I..." I stopped.

"Yooou...?" my therapist coaxed.

"I think I might be exercising too much."

It wasn't much. But it had been something I'd been thinking about.

"How much do you exercise?"

"I run twice a day. Ten miles. That's too much, isn't it?"

"So you run twenty miles a day?"

"No, ten. Five in the morning, five at night."

"Are you training for a marathon?"

"No. Well, yes. Sort of."

"Which is it?"

"I'd like to... I just don't know if I have it in me."

"You run every day?"

"Everyday."

"Mmm..." She jotted something down on the pad in her lap.

"Is it something I should be concerned about?" I said.

"Have you mentioned this to your primary care physician?"

"No... Should I?"

"I was just curious what he had to say."

"Well, I was thinking this was more of a psychological thing rather than a... physical thing."

"I can see where you'd get that idea. I'm not disagreeing with you. I guess the question is: Are you using running as an excuse to avoid other responsibilities or activities such as relationships or engaging in other hobbies or spending time with family and friends?"

I thought about that.

"I see where you're going with this," I said. "It's a good question, too. You wouldn't be too overly upset if I didn't answer that today, would you?"

"It's not my place to be overly upset. I'm a therapist. I'm trained to be impartial."

"That's good; I appreciate that. Because I'm going to have to mull that one over a bit before I give you that very direct and thoughtful response you've come to expect from me."

My therapist winked at me playfully. "I figured as much."

3.

After I got home, I went for a run and I thought about what my therapist had said.

So I made an appointment with my primary care physician.

4.

"So you weren't very specific about your symptoms when you made this appointment," my doc said, consulting his chart. "A general feeling of blah? Can you describe blah for me?"

"Actually, I just told the lady at the appointment desk that so I could see you. I'm really here to get some advice."

You would have thought I'd questioned his oath to keep the sick from harm and injustice by the expression on his face. "You're not sick?" he said.

"No, sir."

He shrugged. "Well, it's your copay," he said, lowering himself onto his stool.

"I know it's not the best use of your time..."

He just stared at me, like, OK, buddy, cut to the chase.

"Well, I was talking to my therapist yesterday..." I waited to see if he was going to react to that but he didn't. He just kept looking at me, challenging me to keep his interest. "I told her I'm pretty fanatical about running and I asked her if she thought I might be over-exercising and one of the first things she wanted to know was, have I talked to you about it? Which I thought was a little strange..."

"Why would you talk to me about it?"

"Exactly."

"How do you feel when you're running?"

"I feel fine."

"No pain? No discomfort?"

"Just the usual aches and..." I was going to say pains but I figured that would have immediately caused him to refer me to a specialist.

"And how often do you run?"

"Twice a day. Ten miles."

"So that's what – twenty miles a day?"

Why was everyone have so much trouble doing the math on that?

"No – ten miles a day. Five in the morning, five at night."

"OK. And what did your therapist say?"

As if that mattered.

"She said it's possible I could be over-exercising if I'm using running as an excuse to avoid other responsibilities."

"That sounds good. I agree. I still don't know why she asked if you'd talked to me about it."

"I don't either."

"Your therapist sounds very insecure. Would you like me to make a referral for you? As long as you're here."

"Look, I'm not unhappy with my therapist. I just really wanted to get a second opinion."

"Well, I can understand that. Don't feel pressured to accept my referral. I mean, that's your call. I was simply extending the offer. Letting you know it's available."

"Thanks. But you're OK with me running twice a day?"

"I have no problem with it."

"As long as..."

"Really sounds like this is something for you and your therapist to hash out. She's much more tuned in to that kind of stuff."

"You think?"

"Oh sure, sure. Definitely."

5.

I needed a drink after that, so I stopped off at Duffy's Tavern and order a Mojito.

"Tough day?" The Duff said.

"They're all tough days, Duff."

The Duff laughed. "You're all roses and sunshine, ain't ya, kid?"

Then I remembered something.

"Duff, let me ask you something. You've taken a few psychology classes."

"Yeah - so I can better understand some of the jerks that come in here."

"What do you think's wrong with me?"

"What do I think?"

"Yeah – best guess."

The Duff studied me intently. In his mind he was paging through all those Into to Psych text books he'd been required to read in high school and the nine community colleges he'd attended over the years. After finding the right chapter and page number, he said, "I think you probably suffered a lot of emotional trauma in your youth."

"Really?"

The Duff shrugged. "Just off the top of my dome."

I processed that.

"You were obviously short; probably skinny as hell, lot of pimples, hardly any friends. How close am I?"

"Closer than I'm willing to admit."

The Duff pumped his fist several times. "Yes! Still got it!"

"You know I didn't kiss a girl until I was twenty-six?" I said.

"It happens."

"And I had to pay to kiss her."

"A hooker?"

"No, it was one of those booths at the county fair. You know, kiss the prettiest girl in town for fifty cents?" I thought about that for a minute. "No wonder I'm in therapy."

The Duff couldn't help but smile.

"And here I am, forty-five years old, never been in a relationship. God, I sound like a serial killer, don't I?"

The Duff patted me on the shoulder. "You're gonna be OK, buddy. You're gonna find somebody. Some guys, it just takes a little longer. You're a late bloomer."

I had to laugh.

People had been calling me a late bloomer since junior high.

I'm not sure who said it first.

My parents, my sister, or one of my teachers.

One of them.

Doesn't really matter at this point.

It was just funny hearing somebody calling me a late bloomer at forty-five.

Guess it sounds better than calling them a failure.

I thanked The Duff for listening to me, gave him a twenty for the drink and told him to keep the change.

6.

During the bus ride back to my apartment, I thought about what The Duff had said.

You know, about me suffering a lot of emotional trauma in my youth and all.

Even though I did get teased a lot for being short and skinny and having a lot of pimples, I had to admit that I teased myself more than anyone else teased me.

And, believe me that can be a whole lot worse.

7.

When I got home I changed into my running clothes and went for a run because running always makes me feel better. It also helps me to process some of my therapist's insights. Like her latest one about using running as an excuse to avoid other aspects of my life.

Now that was deep.

That one kept rolling around inside my head.

It would take more than a few runs for me to be able to sort that one out.

A few miles into the run, I felt my phone vibrating. I usually ignore it, but that time I took it out of my pocket to see who was texting me.

It was Rosalie, bored as hell in her Laguna Beach cottage.

"let's sip Ketel One 2nite like it's your birthday."

The last time Rosalie and I sipped Ketel One like it was my birthday, we ended up at some frat party sipping Everclear with strawberry Kool-Aid like it was my funeral.

"can't," I texted her back. "self-medicating with running," and I turned off my phone and put it back in my pocket.

As I looked ahead toward the horizon, I noticed some kind of glowing, ghostly-lit optical illusion right above it. It made me think of the Flying Dutchman, the legendary phantom ship condemned to sail against the wind until Judgment Day.

That's exactly how I felt.

Adrift at sea, no place to dock, no safe harbor for me.

I looked at my pace watch. That damn 8.5 minute mile was still eluding me. Hadn't been able to get it under 10 ever since I went to that running clinic at the hospital where a licensed physical therapist performed an "initial comprehensive running evaluation" using "state-of-the-art Dartfish video analysis and a force plate treadmill" on me.

"You should focus more on a forefront strike as opposed to a heel strike," the licensed physical therapist said. "And try to keep your strike under your body, aligned with your hips and torso."

So I did.

That day, however, I must not have been focusing enough or something because as I was evaluating my foot strike and whether my hips and torso were properly aligned, I noticed I'd forgotten to double-knot my laces, which were dangling dangerously. When I finally made the decision to stop and retie them, the edge of my right heel caught the lip of a pothole, I lost my balance, spun around, tumbled hard to the pavement, and landed flat on my back.

Most runners would have gotten back up, started running again.

But not me.

I just laid there. Kind of enjoyed it, too, to tell you the truth. Maybe because I knew I was just a little banged-up. Maybe because I just didn't feel like running anymore.

I thought it was interesting; even though I was lying down, I could still see that horizon, only this time there were no illusions; just some light rays shining through clouds.

Then I turned my head slightly to the left and saw my reflection in a puddle of rainwater and immediately thought of Narcissus, because one time my therapist called me "narcissistic".

That's not the face of a narcissus, I thought. That's the face of a man experiencing general malaise and fatigue who's involved in a very long-distance run against himself.

I sort of laughed.

I'll have to remember that line the next time I see my therapist, I thought.

She loves it when I challenge her insights.

I think she'll really get a kick out of it.

So Tired, Mama

Picture this, a man in his late forties, doesn't dress too well, doesn't eat too well, can't maintain a relationship, probably a drinker, pretty much of a loner, sitting there in a tee shirt and underwear and sweat socks, listening to classical music on the local college radio station, head down, about to cry, feeling that thing in his throat, his gut, that thing he gets every time somebody asks him a personal question, every time that happens he feels like running away, doesn't wanna answer any more personal questions, just wants to keep his distance, because he lost a brother to suicide and a mother to cancer and he thinks he's gonna lose somebody else to something or other, so why bother getting close? So he holes himself up in his little room, reading "The Catcher in the Rye" and drinking whiskey, walking that damn tightrope, wanting, needing solitude, but imprisoned by his loneliness. Another year gone and he still refuses to make eye contact with humanity. Just keeps looking down at the sidewalk. Avoiding everybody. Everywhere.

Happiness Is...

Another one of those words - like faith - that has become utterly
meaningless. Happiness is just another manufactured concept. It's
something *else* they try to sell us on. Like religion and democracy and
tooth whitener. Anybody who tells you that life is satisfying is a
mental paralytic. The Buddhists have it about half right. Because a
Buddhist knows how shitty life really is. A Buddhist is honest
enough to admit there is only the present and trying to go forward or
backward in time is not only a monumental waste of time, it causes
increased pain and dis-ease and dissatisfaction and eventually leads to
physical and psychological damage. Science bears this out. Hell, *I*
bear this out. If I continually go back, revisit those memories of me
as a child, everything about me changes. My mood, my posture, the
muscles in my face. And I'll prove this to you. Now, I'm not an actor.
I'm not making any of this up. I haven't even gotten this shit I'm
about to share with you down on paper. But it's all up here. It's *still*
up here. I'm hoping one day medical science will create a form of
dynamite for the mind which will allow us to demolish all those bad
memories we don't want to think about anymore. That'd be great.
Nevertheless. It's obvious I got a lot of anger, right? Lot of
bitterness. Frustration. Hopelessness, yeah, I got very little faith in
you, in me, in any of us. Call me what you will. I don't give a damn.
What the fuck difference does it make? Am I depressed? Of course.
Aren't you? I'd be worried about you if you weren't. So you would
prefer I smile more. Crack a few more jokes. Stop being so serious.
Lighten up. That's *your* hang-up. If I bring you down, then leave me
the hell alone. It's very simple. You don't have to be around me. It's
quite likely I don't wanna be around you, anyway, so, do yourself a
favor and keep it moving. I see some of you are laughing. You think
I'm joking. I'm not joking. This is what I believe. It's what I've
always believed. I'm not a fucking comedian. I'm a guy whose
mother decided she'd be better off leaving me in a foster home so
she could continue to drink herself to death. I can't say I blame her.
We all gotta go sometime. We all gotta die *of* something. Might as
well be of our own choosing. Might as well take control of the
motherfucker, in my opinion. So, yeah, those of you out there trying
to psychoanalyze me, knock yourselves out. There's a lot to
psychoanalyze, trust me. I'm just getting started, so... Two or three
more whiskeys and anything can happen. I got lucky. I learned to

string a few words together. Some people actually read what I wrote and didn't go blind in the process. I'm what they call a cult writer. The egg heads and the New York critics hate me. And they can all go fuck themselves. They're not fit to wipe my ass. I'm one of those rare individuals who doesn't give a rat's ass about making money. I make enough to keep just the right percentage of alcohol in my blood. That's pretty much all I care about at this point in my life. Most people think I've chosen to throw up my hands. And I have. I'm tired. At some point you just become tired of all the bullshit. Another day, another holiday, another birthday, another death day. Another bill, another trip to the doctor, another car repair, another murder, another political campaign, another war. It's endless... And yet we're continually told to buck up, stay strong, laugh through the pain, endure. When the chips are down, when the going gets tough... God bless the American Spirit. I'm not a lonely man. I find this country, in particular, has a real problem with those who prefer to be alone. I don't need camaraderie. I don't have to go bowling or fishing or go to church. I don't need to bond with my fellow man or woman or have a shared experience of any kind. If history teaches us anything about the human being it is that he is a complete failure. This has been proven time and time again. The human being can't even get along with himself, let alone others. The only, the *only* redeeming quality the human being possesses is that he will one day die. That is the *only* redeeming quality. Do I believe in God? Well...the only reasonable, logical, intelligent response to a question like that is I don't know. If people were honest enough with themselves and with each other, which they will never be... every last bloody one of them would come to that conclusion. There is a not a single man, woman, or child on this bitch of an earth who can answer that question with any real certainty. The Atheists are wrong. The believers are wrong. The Buddhists are about half right. The Jews about an eighth right; maybe a quarter right. The Christians and the Catholics are flat-out delusional. The Muslims, who the hell knows what they believe? And the Jehovah Witnesses and the Mormons, Christ, you might as well just join the circus.

ABOUT THE AUTHOR

Phloyd Knucklez makes you think of a hunting tiger. He has hooded sapphire eyes. He is bald, but used to have thick, straight hair the color of polished amber He is very short and has a narrow build. His skin is china-white. He has thin lips. His wardrobe is dignified and plain, with a lot of red.